TAKE CARE OF OLD SQUIRE

LINDSEY THORNTON

All rights reserved. No part of this book shall be reproduced or transmitted in any form or by any means, electronic, mechanical, magnetic, photographic including photocopying, recording or by any information storage and retrieval system, without prior written permission of the publisher. No patent liability is assumed with respect to the use of the information contained herein. Although every precaution has been taken in the preparation of this book, the publisher and author assume no responsibility for errors or omissions. Neither is any liability assumed for damages resulting from the use of the information contained herein.

Copyright © 2002 by Lindsey Thornton

ISBN 978-0-7414-1177-8

Printed in the United States of America

This is a work of fiction. Names, characters, places, and incidents either are the product of the author's imagination or are used fictitiously. Any resemblance to actual events or locales or persons, living or dead, is entirely coincidental.

INFINITY PUBLISHING
1094 New DeHaven Street, Suite 100
West Conshohocken, PA 19428-2713
Toll-free (877) BUY BOOK
Local Phone (610) 941-9999
Fax (610) 941-9959
Info@buybooksontheweb.com
www.buybooksontheweb.com

DEDICATION

This book is dedicated to my husband, children, and grandchildren, who loved and supported me as I took time to write this story, and to other family members and special friends, who believed in this story and helped to make the book a reality.

Chapter One

Sylvia pulled into the driveway, and gazed through the windshield of her car. So hard to believe it was her house. All through college she'd dreamed of the day she could leave her dingy little apartment. She lowered the car window, and enjoyed the moment. She'd worked hard to finish school and save money for the down payment. Writing the checks the day before had made everything a reality, a new veterinary practice, and a house.

Sylvia had been offered a partnership with two fellow graduates who were going for the high-end customers near Atlanta, but she wanted to be closer to home. She'd always loved the small town atmosphere in Kinsey. She'd heard stories of her mother being related to the Kinsey family, but couldn't confirm the stories. Her mother's parents were killed in an accident and she'd grown up in her maternal grandparents home. The Kinsey connection would've been on her father's side, and she'd never seen them. Sylvia's father was from Kinsey, and his family all lived within two miles of each other. Her parents met somewhere near Athens, Georgia when the fair came to town in nineteen thirty-six. They married, and made Kinsey their home. Sylvia couldn't imagine living anywhere else. She was glad to be home.

Sylvia opened the car door, stepped out, and waved to a neighbor in the distance. It appeared to be an older woman, she couldn't be sure. The area was so inviting. Happy houses, all facing the highway, were nestled among the old pecan trees. Once plantation land, everyone on the highway shared a piece of the old orchard. Sylvia had purchased five acres and the old house, circa nineteen thirties. Somehow, she'd known as soon as she saw the yellow frame house with white shutters, that it would be perfect for her. The old house had been closed up for years and needed some restoration, but fit her budget and nostalgic nature. She was sure the old place would be livable, after a few weeks of hard work.

Sylvia gathered what boxes she could handle, and made her way to the front steps. The old wooden boards moaned as if in pain from the weight of her footsteps. Inside, she opened the old windows, and a cool breeze kept her company as she scrubbed the wood floors. It was late into the night when she realized that exhaustion had taken over. She opened the canvas cot, which she'd borrowed from her mother, threw on a sheet, and quickly fell asleep.

Chapter Two

The sun's rays, dancing on the mirror over the old mantle, awakened Sylvia. She turned on her hot plate and boiled some water for coffee. Realizing there was nowhere to sit anything, she searched the house. She looked into the dark little closet in the hallway, and found an old piece of shelving. As she removed it from the brackets, an envelope fell to the floor. She reached down to pick it up. No name or address and an open flap, the envelope was inviting. The paper inside was brittle, so she carefully unfolded the creasing, trying not to tear it. Written in shaky handwriting, were the words: "Take care of Old Squire." No explanation, and no signature. As she was placing the note back in the envelope, there was a knock at the front door. She threw the envelope onto the top shelf, and ran to answer.

Envisioning an older man in overalls, she was instantly embarrassed! Here stood a Greek god with paintbrush in hand!

"Good morning. You're the painter, right? Please excuse my appearance. I've been trying to get some cleaning done. Come in."

"Alright. I've got a couple of guys who'll be here shortly."

"Would you like some coffee while you wait?"

"Don't drink the stuff." he replied

"I only drink decaffeinated, and only one cup in the mornings. I don't really know why. Guess its just habit."

Remembering that decaffeinated coffee wasn't habit forming, she hushed before embarrassing herself further. He said nothing, just walked around the room looking at the peeling paint.

"We'll need to caulk the window panes too." she said

"Oh? I didn't realize that you were going to help us!"

How very rude she thought, but remembered that most men who looked like him, were rude. His helpers arrived, and he left the room to give instructions. Sylvia chose the paint samples, and decided to make herself scarce.

"I'll be working in the kitchen if you need anything. I don't want to get in the way."

"That'd probably be best!" he replied

Sylvia concentrated on the old kitchen sinks. She mixed chlorine bleach, powdered cleanser, and pine cleaner. She was quickly overcome by the fumes, and fainted. She woke up when someone wiped her face with a cool cloth. She noticed an odor of sweet hay in the room. When able, she pulled herself from the floor and looked around the room. There was no one there. She went into the front room. All three painters were busy scraping and painting.

"Excuse me, did anyone go into the kitchen?" she asked

"Nope. We'll do one room at a time, Lady!" Mr. Rudeness replied

She knew someone had put a cloth on her face. She went back to the kitchen. There was no cloth, and the smell was gone! Deciding that it was her imagination, she went back to work, using one cleanser at a time.

Sylvia admired her work, and thought of her grandmother's old sinks. Hers had been the same kind before she remodeled a few years back. She remembered baby's being bathed, corn being scraped, and mountains of dishes being washed in them.

By four o'clock that afternoon, the front room was painted. One of the helpers appeared in the kitchen doorway.

"Hey, we're leaving. Can we wash up at the spigot outside?"

"Sure. You'll be back tomorrow to start in here, won't you?"

"Seven o'clock, Ma'am."

"Have a nice evening, and thanks for the hard work today. Is your boss gone?"

"Yeah. See you tomorrow."

Finally alone, Sylvia went to take a bath. She turned on both faucets and sat on the side of the old claw-foot tub, letting the water run over her fingertips. The water was cool and soothing, but she soon realized it wasn't becoming any warmer. Reaching for the sink, she tried the hot faucet and also found cold water there. Tired and in need of bath, she had no choice but to go to her parents for the night. Sleeping in her old bedroom was a comforting thought after a tiring day.

After dinner and a long bath, Sylvia crawled into bed.

"Honey" her dad called "I'll send someone tomorrow to check the hot water heater for you. Hope there's not a lot of surprise repairs over there you didn't count on."

"Maybe not, Dad. I'm going to sleep now. Thanks for the help. Tell Mom thanks too. I'm not sure if I thanked her for dinner."

Within minutes, she fell asleep. The next day would be a busy one for her.

Chapter Three

Sylvia officially hung the shingle at her clinic. Orders had been placed for tables, medical supplies, kennels, and an x-ray machine. She couldn't take on patients until everything arrived, but had plenty of cleaning to keep her busy.

The rooms of the clinic were small, but adequate. Sylvia opened the back door of the building to find little space for a dog run, and no fence. She laughed to herself at the thought of confronting her dad with "hidden expenses."

She was cleaning the hallway when she heard a child calling from the front of the building.

"Please, help me!"

She found a freckled faced child standing in the doorway. A limp puppy dangled from the little boy's arms.

"My mama said he ain't breathing! She said you'd fix him if you was open yet."

Sylvia took the puppy, while explaining that she had no supplies on hand. The puppy was breathing, but faintly. Laying the puppy on his side, she administered short thrust. Out popped a bottle cap!

"Here's your problem. The cap was stuck in his airway!"

The little boy's face lit up as he heard the puppy try to bark.

"Thanks Lady! My mama said to tell me how much we owe, and she'll pay you on Friday. She don't have no money today. What's your name?"

"I'm Dr. Champion. Since I'm not really open for business, and you are my first client, you owe me nothing. Promise not to play with small objects around your puppy again. Use a tennis ball. He can't swallow one of those, okay?"

"Okay. I'll tell my mama to buy me one. Thanks."

The child ran home with his puppy. Sylvia felt proud that she had helped him.

The painters were near finishing the kitchen by the time she arrived home.

"Hey, you look better today!" the painter said "You clean up good. Oh yeah, the hot water heater was out. Repairman left the ticket on the counter. He installed a new one."

"Thank you. Can we go over painting plans for the bedrooms? I'm not sure the colors I have in mind will blend."

"You thought you hired a designer? You pick the colors; we put them on the wall. That's how it works! I need a decision. I've gotta pick up the paint before the store closes today."

"Fine! Just get off white."

Although aggravated by his sarcasm, Sylvia was impressed with the work he'd done. The walls of the kitchen had a faint tint of lavender over white. She envisioned an airy wicker table and chairs, and white lace curtains, which would allow the morning sun to flow through the room into the hallway. "Country kitchen" she whispered

The painter called out from the hallway.

"Hey, we're outta here for today."

She walked into where he was standing, to make one more attempt at being nice.

"Okay, thanks for a great job. By the way, what's your name?"

"Chuck."

Sylvia watched as he removed his coveralls, exposing Levis and Tee shirt. Embarrassed, she quickly looked away and said good-bye.

From the door she could see that the sun was going down. Sylvia found an old crate, put it out on the porch, and sat down. She had a clear view of the sunset in the distance, and watched as the sky turned from pale blue to brilliant shades of red and orange. The sound of a mini bike startled her, and she turned to see two boys riding near the highway's edge.

"Hello" she called out

They stopped, hearing her voice.

"Hey, you movin' in that old house?"

"I'm working on it!"

"You know it's haunted? That's what my uncle said. He lives down the road. Mrs. Cotton used to live there. She was nuts!"

They said bye, and sped away.

"Haunted house?" she laughed

She found the notion fascinating. Her mind drifted back to the ghost stories told by her grandmother. There were tales of windows opening by themselves, chains being dragged around the house, and even a ghost dog who reportedly led an uncle to a hidden treasure. She'd never believed the stories, but found them entertaining as a child. She was amused at the thought of her house spurring such tales for other children.

The sun disappeared, so Sylvia went inside. She ran a nice hot bath and was just about to step in, when she heard a knock at the door. Dressed only in her robe, she opened the door to find Chuck.

"Hi, did you leave something?" she asked

"No. I thought I'd invite you out to eat. I've noticed you don't have a stove. I guess you were ready for bed, huh?"

"No, just about to get a shower. I'd like to go if you could give me about thirty minutes. I'm not exactly dressed for dinner."

"I can run to the post office and drop off some mail. I'll be back in thirty minutes."

"I'll be ready."

Sylvia quickly bathed, blew her hair dry, and tried on three outfits before deciding what to wear. She was ready by the time he returned.

"Where are we going?"

"Not many choices in this town, you know. You like seafood?"

"That's fine with me."

The restaurant was crowded. They were seated in a corner next to a table of enthusiastic hunters. There would be a wait for food, the waitress announced. Sylvia tried to ignore the conversation coming from the hunter's table until her meal arrived.

"Food alright?" Chuck asked
"What?"
"The food. Is it okay?" he yelled
"Yes, fine."

Conversation ceased. They couldn't hear above the crowd noise. After dinner, Chuck suggested a drive to the river. They talked as they rode down the bumpy back roads.

"Sorry 'bout the restaurant. I didn't know they'd be so busy." he said

"No problem, really. Can I ask you something?"
"Okay."
"Why have you given me such a hard time?"
"Hard time?"
"You've been rude, given me short answers, made me feel stupid, etc. etc."

"I guess I figured you wrong to start with. I really thought you'd be more uppity. You went to college, and you're a doctor."

"Uppity? You know who my dad is. He's run that old hardware store all my life. We've never been uppity people!"

"Okay, I'm sorry. Honesty counts for something don't it? I mean I could've said I didn't know what you's talking about. I admit I was sort'a rude! I see you ain't so uppity now."

Sylvia laughed.

The moonlight danced on the water, as they watched from the old ferry landing.

"Somethin' wrong? You looked like you were a million miles away."

"No. Actually I was right here. This place holds a lot of memories for me. I came here as a kid with my brothers. Once, we brought our tent and camped right over there by the willow tree. When we woke the next morning, Mom and Dad were parked on the hill behind us. They'd slept in their car."

"Worried I guess. Sounds like you had good folks. Mine were just happy when I was out of the house."

"I'm really thankful for my parents. Sometimes I fail to show them how much I appreciate all they've done. I guess I need to work on that!"

"Ever fish out here?"

"Sure! I always out fished my brothers. Of course, they wouldn't tell you that."

It was late, and Sylvia needed to rise early the next morning. They rode back to her house. As they pulled into the driveway, she turned to Chuck.

"It's been a nice evening. Thanks for dinner, and the drive."

"Hey, I was surprised, myself!"

That night she lay in bed thinking of him. His face was becoming familiar. He had very strong features, and dark, long eyelashes. His hair had a slight wave, but wouldn't be considered curly, she thought. She tried to put a name to the color. It wasn't blonde, but not quite brown either. It was somewhere in-between. Dishwater blonde didn't sound right for a guy. His eyes were definitely blue, and deeply sensitive when he spoke. She'd have to be careful, she thought. She was much too attracted.

Chapter Four

The clinic was shaping up by Thursday. Sylvia held interviews for an assistant and a receptionist. Recently graduated from high school, Marty would work through the summer while deciding on his major. He was a cute kid with dark hair and eyes. His enthusiasm was overwhelming, and Sylvia was impressed with his feelings toward animals. Mechelle was chosen for the receptionist position. Tall, with dark hair, she was attending college at night toward an accounting degree. She was polite, seemed genuine, and was full of optimism about her future.

By Friday the office was stocked, and Mechelle had scheduled four minor surgeries for the next week. Sylvia had worried that it might take a year for her business to flourish. She assumed that it would take that long for people to begin to trust her, and was happy that things were looking hopeful so quickly.

During the first days in business, there'd been comments about female veterinarians. Sylvia usually gave a polite acknowledgement of the statements, and went about her business. She knew that times were changing for women, but some were slow to accept the changes. She'd dealt with discrimination from some of the older professors in college, and was well prepared for any farmer's comments.

Marty had been a good decision. His patience and genuine sense of compassion for the patients, was amazing. The animals seemed at ease in his presence. Sylvia was quick to praise his good work.

"You're giving me the big head" he said, "I just hope I can live up to all of this praise."

"Me too! That was my strategy," she said jokingly

Chuck called the clinic to make sure Sylvia's house would be open on Saturday morning.

"I'll leave the key...no wait a minute. The floor refinishing is scheduled for Saturday. Can you work around them?"

"No, I'd better wait. I'll see you on Tuesday if that's alright."

"Sure. I'll see you then."

She was disappointed. Until then, he hadn't called since their dinner date. He didn't mention the date or ask to see her again, other than to work on her house. She closed up, and went home.

Sylvia busied herself putting shelf liner in the kitchen cabinets. As she was cleaning the scrap paper from the floor, she caught a whiff of the strange smell of sweet hay again. She tried to follow the scent. It became neither stronger nor weaker wherever she walked in the room. As quickly as it had appeared, it was gone. She reasoned that it must have been something in the old walls or the cellar, perhaps some odor drawn through the room on a breeze from the open window.

The telephone rang, startling her.

"Hello."

"Want'a grab a pizza?"

It was Chuck.

"I'm a mess. How long do I have to get ready?"

There was a knock in the front of the house.

She walked into the hallway and listened.

"Can you hang on a minute?"

"Somethin' wrong?"

"Someone's knocking."

She opened the front door, but found no one there. As she closed the door, there was another knock. This one came from behind her. She ran back to the phone.

"Chuck? Come on over. I'll be ready when you get here."

"You got company?"

"No. I guess I just thought I heard someone at the door. Hurry on over!"

"You sure?"

"Yeah, I'm sure!"

She brushed her hair, washed up, and listened for more knocks. They'd stopped. Chuck arrived with pizza, wine and candles.

"How sweet," she said

"I figured you'd be tired. Got any glasses around here?"

"Only paper cups. Sorry."

"Only cheap wine. It's alright," he laughed

They sat on a blanket to eat. He smiled as a cheese string clung to her chin, and gently wiped it away with a napkin.

"Have you ever heard any strange stories about this house being haunted?" she asked

"No, why? Have you seen a ghost?"

"Not exactly."

She told him what the two boys on the bike had said, and mentioned the mysterious knocking, and the strange feeling of someone wiping her face the day she'd fainted.

"I don't believe in spirits, but it's pretty weird. It does scare me a little."

"Probably the old pipes. Old things make some pretty strange noises. How's the plumbin' in this place?"

"I'm having everything replaced that's not up to code. You're probably right. I'm just being silly."

Chuck lay back on the blanket and pulled her next to him. She felt safe. He talked of plans to buy a Harley and travel across the country. She lay quietly listening to his stories and tried to envision riding on the back of a Harley, her hair flying in the wind. Never the adventurous type, she couldn't imagine that it would ever happen. Noticing the time, he prepared to leave. She hadn't realized how long they'd been talking.

"You ain't bad company," he said

"Thanks, I think! I really enjoyed the conversation. So I'll see you on Tuesday?"

Chuck nodded, then leaned over and kissed her forehead.

"Sorry I kept you so late." she said

"I'm not." he answered as he approached his truck.

Chapter Five

For the next two weeks, everything was busy. The house was nearly ready for furniture, and the clinic was hectic. Farmers began calling about house calls for larger animals.
"Who took care of the rural animals before I came? The traveling vet died three years ago!"
"I'm not sure," Mechelle answered "The nearest vet is thirty-two miles away. I guess some people just treated their own."
"We need to work out a different schedule for the rural clients. What if we make the house call appointments on one day each week? I'll let you work it out. Whatever you can come up with, starting next week."
"I'll handle it. I know it's been tough on you. Have you even bought any furniture for your house?"
"No. I just haven't had time."
"Maybe this weekend, huh?"
"Maybe. Thanks for your help with the scheduling."
On Saturday morning, Sylvia did go shopping. She found an old sofa in need of re-stuffing and new fabric, but perfect for the house.
"Do you have anyone you could recommend for upholstery?" Sylvia asked the shop owner.
"We use the little shop on the corner. We'll be happy to send it over for you. You'll need to go by and select your fabric, but I'll call ahead for you."
She went from shop to shop searching for anything resembling nineteen thirty décor. She found one bedroom suite in mint condition. The wood was beautifully carved and the original springs were optional with purchase. She chose to take them. The owner of the shop located another similar bedroom suite, and promised to have it within ten days.

Sylvia made it home by four-thirty. She unloaded the car of small items she'd purchased. While struggling with the television stand and the front door, she heard someone offer assistance. She turned to find a mail carrier.

"Let me help you little lady."

"Thanks so much! I thought I could handle it, but see I can't. Aren't you working a little late?"

"Just finishin' up. Saturdays always a long day. You like it here okay?"

She opened the door and he sat the stand inside.

"I love the place. It'll be good as new when the remodeling is complete."

"You're the new animal doc aren't you?"

"I'm sorry, yes. Sylvia Champion. And you are?"

"Mr. Abernathy. It's good to have somebody livin' here again. House always looked sad just sittin' here empty."

"Well, I hate to cut this short, but I really need to get busy inside. It was nice to meet you, and thanks for the help."

"You ain't seen Squire around have you?"

"Who?"

"Mrs. Cotton lived here for years. I think the Cotton's built this house. Anyhow, she swore she had a ghost named Squire livin' here. We always humored her. She watton in good health, you know. I never did meet Mr. Cotton. He'd been dead a while when I took this route."

"I have no ghost stories for you Mr. Abernathy."

As Sylvia went into the house, she thought of the note she'd found her first day in the house. The note had said Old Squire. So he was Mrs. Cotton's imaginary friend. Probably old, she thought, because Mrs. Cotton was old herself. The boys had called her crazy, but Sylvia found it sad. She imagined that the woman made up a friend after her husband died... someone to spend time with.

The furniture truck arrived with the bedroom suite and television. Sylvia put the old bed together, pulled the springs over the slats, and added the new mattress. It was as high as her grandmother Champion's old bed. She sat on the edge of the bed, and bounced. Fresh new sheets in colors of mint green and white, fell gracefully in the air as she flipped them above the bed. Adding a cream-colored chenille spread with a mint flower in the center completed the bed. The antique green boudoir lamp with tiny fringe, made the room true thirties.

Within ten days the second bedroom had been furnished. She chose colors in rose and white for that room. Her grandmother gifted her with an antique coverlet for the bed. The tiny sweet heart roses, embroidered on the white background, added warmth to the room and would invite her sleep over guest. The sofa arrived and was just what she had imagined. The upholstery print in colors of blue and rose had set the tone for the front room. She hung blue sheers, which flowed over the windows and allowed filtered light to spill into the room. A large oval rug in a dusty rose color with blue edging was rolled out onto the floor. A refurbished floor lamp in the corner, a few candles on the mantle, two crystal candy dishes on the side tables, and the room was done.

She'd found the perfect wicker table and chairs for the kitchen, and ordered them express shipping from a catalog. The cushions were custom sewn by her mother in a print of spring colored morning glories. She was excited to see the old house come alive, but still had made no decision on the exterior paint. After carefully staring from every possible angle, she could make no changes. The house had invited her because of the colors, so she told the painters to repaint with pale yellow and trim in white. She added a porch swing, painted white.

The house was charming, but pulling into the drive each day Sylvia felt that something was missing. Mr. Abernathy delivered the mail one afternoon while she was sitting on the porch swing.

"You gonna put the fence back up?"

"There wasn't a fence when I bought the place."

"No, it's been gone a while. Guess the realty folks didn't want to fix it."

"Was it a picket fence?"

"Yeah. Always looked real nice when it was kep' up."

"I knew something was missing! I kept trying to figure what else the house needed. I think you're right. I might look into having one built. Thanks."

"I could help you with that. I do some woodwork in my spare time. Pretty good at it too!"

"That'd be great! Just let me know what materials you need."

"I'll take some measurements and get up a list. I gotta go right now though. I'll see ya about it later."

"Thank you, Mr. Abernathy."

Chapter Six

Sylvia was seeing more of Chuck. She invited him for dinner at least twice a week. One night while sitting in the front room, Chuck noticed that the clock had the incorrect time. He brought it to her attention.

"I've reset the darn thing everyday! I don't know what the problem is. I had it all through college and it kept perfect time."

He reset the clock to read eight-thirty. Later they noticed it had gone back to six o'clock.

"I think it's time to get a new clock, Sylvia!"

"I'll have it looked at. I hate to get rid of it. Mom gave it to me when I left home."

Chuck left to go home and Sylvia placed the clock by her purse on the table. She had plans to meet Mr. Abernathy to purchase materials for the fence the next afternoon, and would drop it off on the way.

News of Vietnam was always the topic of conversation in town. Every client, the clock repairman, and Mr. Abernathy all discussed the war. Sylvia worried about her younger brother, David. He was eligible for the draft. She tried not to think of him ever going overseas. He'd worked at the hardware store since his early teens and loved the business. Her dad depended on him so much. Sylvia's older brother, Matt, made it past the draft. He was thirty, married with two children, and living in Athens. He was a financial advisor. They'd not been close for several years with her away at school, him living in another town. She hated conversations of war. Each one caused her to go through a mental list of friends and family again. So many young men were being sent to the jungle. She wasn't sure why.

Sylvia made a stop by the clinic to check for emergency calls. Marty was there alone.

"Had any problems or calls while I was out?"

"No, everything went fine."

The telephone rang and Marty went to answer.

"Dr. Champion, you'd better take this. The guy sounds upset."

"This is Dr. Champion, can I help you?"

"I've got a quarter horse that's really sick. He's not eating, and he's got fever. He's been like this since yesterday and I'm worried!"

"Okay, give me a location and I'll come out."

"He's on a trailer headed in from Alabama. My brother's pulling the trailer. Could he bring him by your place?"

"Sure. What time would he arrive?"

"About an hour, I think. I have a number to call him back with directions. We'll be there in a little while."

"Sir, what's your name?"

"I'm sorry. Michael Ellis."

"We'll see you here."

Marty was asked to stay and help. They prepared a rolling cart with necessary items. Chuck called to ask when Sylvia would be closing up.

"Late. I have an emergency coming in."

"Dog get run over?"

"No, it's a horse on a trailer. You can come help if you want. You might pick up a burger for me and Marty, if you don't mind."

"I don't know how much I could help, but I'll bring you somethin' to eat. Where you gonna put a horse?"

"I'll just check him on the trailer. They're not from here."

"Oh I see. I'll be there after while."

Chuck and Mr. Ellis arrived, and everyone went into the clinic to wait. Sylvia could see that the owner was pacing the floor.

"Mr. Ellis, there's coffee in the back if you want."

"No thanks. They should be here soon."

She didn't want to show self-doubt, but she had some. She was still new in the field of larger animals and had only assisted with serious cases in college. She prayed she'd know what to do.

The trailer arrived, and Sylvia climbed into the stall. Marty fastened a light to the wall as Sylvia stroked the horse's head. She was impressed with his beauty. His coat was deeply black, and glistened with blue highlights. He had a full mane of thick braided hair, and wonderful muscle tone. She could see weakness in his eyes, upon closer examination. His coat felt damp, and he was feverish.

"We need to get him out of this trailer. I can't run test in close quarters. His breathing is labored, and his heart rate is elevated!"

"Is he okay, though?"

"No Mr. Ellis, he's not. How far is your stable?"

"East Coast."

Sylvia knew she had to take the horse somewhere. Her parent's neighbors, Jeremy and Lisa came to mind. No, she remembered, they were away for a month.

"I don't know where we can take him. I'll check my files and call some of the rural customers."

"Sylvia, what about your place?" Chuck suggested "It's dry and not too far from here."

"I didn't even think of it! Follow me with the trailer, Mr. Ellis. Marty, you go and help unload the horse; then come back for supplies. Chuck, can you round up some straw for bedding? I'm sure there isn't anything in that old barn."

"I'll get the straw. You go ahead, and I'll meet you out there."

The horse was unloaded. Chuck arrived with the straw, and Marty helped spread it in the best stall. Sylvia started an IV and took blood samples. Mr. Ellis and his brother were pacing and constantly asking questions. She was losing her patience.

"Where can I reach you? There's no need in everyone staying. I'll do my best, and call with any changes."

"I guess the local motel in town. I'll have to get the number for you. Are you sure I don't need to stay? I'd want to be here if anything bad happened."

"You go. I'll call if he gets into danger. Don't worry about the number. I can get it. Try not to worry!"

Marty was sent to Athens with the blood samples. After starting fluids and injecting medication thought appropriate, Sylvia went to the house to gather blankets and a pillow. She changed into comfortable clothes for what looked to be a long night.

The horse was showing no improvement. Sylvia sent Chuck back to the clinic with a list of needed supplies. She soaked sponges and wet the horse down. His fever had increased. Unless the blood test showed internal infection, she had no clue where the fever was coming from. She made several inspections of possible sights for infections and found nothing! Chuck returned, and she administered another antibiotic.

"I like to watch you work. You really care about animals, don't you?"

"I love my work, but I'm really worried about this horse! I'll be glad when Marty gets back."

"Come over here and sit down. You just gave him that medicine. It might start workin' in a few minutes."

The medication wasn't working. Chuck was dozing off near ten o'clock. Sylvia woke him.

"Please go on home. There's nothing you can do, and you have to work tomorrow. No sense in both of us losing sleep."

"You'll call if you need anything?"

"Yes. Now go home!"

Marty returned with bad news. The lab couldn't get the results until morning. Sylvia became more concerned. Not wanting Marty to see her lack of confidence, she convinced him to leave. Alone with no clue of what to do, she thought of her college textbooks. Armed with three large manuals she pulled from her closet, she ran back to the barn to read. After reading for two hours, she could find nothing to contradict what she'd done. She began to cry, and out of frustration she yelled.

"I don't know what else to do! God I need help!"

After composing herself, she walked back to the horse. Fever still present, he was barely able to stand. She wet the sponges again and wiped him down.

"Easy boy. It's okay. It's okay."

Sylvia turned to put the sponge away and caught a glimpse of someone near the barn door. Frightened, she yelled out.

"Who's there? What do you want?"

An old black man stepped into the light. His clothing was well worn, and appeared to be quite wrinkled.

"Sir? Where did you come from? What do you want here? My husband will be back in a few minutes. You'd better go on now!"

The old man walked toward the horse stall, and for a moment said nothing. Sylvia made her way to the barn door in case she needed to run. He stood looking at the sick horse.

"Haws reel sick, Chille. Wat' you doin' wid em?"

"He belongs to a client. I'm a veterinarian and I'm trying to get his fever down. Do you know about horses Mister?"

"My job, tendin' hawses. Ten cows too. Mostly hawses doe. You ain't doin' dis haws no good."

"I'm the vet!" she said defensively

"Don't know bout dat, jest know bout hawses. Dis one dyin' wid poison!"

She knew the old man was right. The horse was dying. She tried to explain everything she'd done, and the old man just laughed. He didn't seem to understand anything she said. If he'd tended horses, she guessed it would have been years before.

"He got poison in dis laig. I know dat!"

"I see nothing swollen or discolored on his legs. I've checked all of them. I know he has fever, if that's what you refer to as poison! I just can't find the source of infection."

"You ain't gone see lesson you cut bove' dis bone. Cut it, you see."

She was so desperate she began listening to the man. She took a scalpel from her bag, and carefully made an incision as instructed. A mass of infection poured from a cyst behind the muscle. She cleaned the area, placed a drain inside, and increased the antibiotic drip.

"Need willow root!"

"This antibiotic will do fine."

"You don't listen a fokes! Come wid me."

He motioned for her to follow him out the barn door into the darkness. She wasn't sure why she did, but realized that she was no longer afraid of the old man. He led her to a tree and instructed her to dig up some of the root.

"This is crazy!"

"Wanna save dat haws don't ya? He be good by moanin' if you put dis on em."

They took the root back to the barn. She prepared a paste from the scrapings, applied the paste to the wound, and wrapped it.

She turned to the old man.

"How did you know, Mister?"

"Jest knowed. I seen it fo'. Why you working wid hawses? You need jest cook an' leave hawses lone."

"I told you, I'm a doctor. Thanks for your help. You can go now. It's late, and I'm sure someone must be looking for you."

"My Molly. Cain't find her nowhere. I stay wid dis haws rite now doe."

"Suit yourself."

Sylvia lied down on her blanket and soon fell asleep. When she awoke, the horse was nearly back to normal. The fever had broken, and he was standing steady. She realized the old man was gone and felt badly for speaking short to him. He'd said he was from near by. She thought perhaps she could find him later.

Sylvia called Mr. Ellis and reported the good news.

"You can pick him up after today. He needs to rest before traveling. Visits are fine if you want to come by."

"Thanks so much. I've been up most of the night."

"Me too!"

Thankful the ordeal was over, Sylvia went in to take a bath and enjoy a cup of coffee. She didn't know if she would tell anyone about the old man. She could imagine what her dad would say after learning that all of the money spent on college hadn't brought the knowledge the old man possessed without benefit of education.

Chapter Seven

Sylvia would often think of the old man. She wasn't sure what led him to the barn. If he was concerned for horses, she reasoned, perhaps a light in the barn so late signaled a problem. She didn't think he could live far since he appeared to be on foot. She hoped to find him, and offer some gratuity for his help.

She did mention the old man to Chuck a few days later, and tried to explain how helpful he'd been.

"Didn't your folks warn you about strangers? He could be dangerous, Sylvia!"

"Oh please! He's an old man. He knows about horses, and even though his treatments are primitive, they worked. My grandmother still uses herbs and some tonics made from plants. Maybe he just happened along at the right time, I don't know. I just want to thank him for saving the horse."

"You don't take any credit?"

"I did what I knew to do and it wasn't enough. He found the infection, I didn't."

"Did you get his name?"

"No. I was so worried about the horse, I didn't even ask."

"I wouldn't worry about it. The old guy probably feels good about being able to help. That aughta be enough."

Sylvia dropped the subject before becoming upset. Chuck didn't understand, and she wasn't going to try explaining her feelings.

Sylvia stopped by her nearest neighbor's one afternoon. She hoped the neighbor would know the old man or where he might live, as there weren't many houses along the highway within walking distance.

As she walked up the stone path to the front of the house, Sylvia noticed a large bed of touch-me-not flowers.

She thought of how many times she'd been in trouble with her grandmother for wasting her seed when she popped the seedpods of her flowers. She knocked several times on the door before someone answered. An old woman appeared.

"What you want?"

"I'm your neighbor, Sylvia Champion. I haven't had time before today to come by and introduce myself."

The door slowly opened and the woman stepped out.

"Mr. Abernathy said a woman doctor moved in the old Cotton place. What kind of doctor are you?"

"A veterinarian. Do you have dogs or cats?"

"No. Cain't take care of animals no more. Takes all my strength to take care of myself. It's nice to have a neighbor though. My names Ella. I'm here most of the time. Kids all grown up and moved away. Lost my husband fifteen years ago. I got church friends that come when they can. You got a church?"

"My parents go every Sunday. I did when I was younger, but I haven't decided where to go now that I'm grown. What church do you attend?"

"It's a little country Baptist church down at Browns Crossroads. You'd be welcome there. Mostly old folks now though. You heard the stories about your house?"

"Yes Ma'am, but I'm not much for ghost stories."

"I didn't never believe it, but some folks talked about it like it was real."

"Yes Ma'am."

"Where you from?"

"Oh, I'm from here. Well, east of town. My parents still live out that way."

"Who's your folks?"

"Jim and Diana Champion. My dad runs the old hardware store down town."

"I know your daddy! My husband used to trade with him. They swapped some big fish stories in that store! Your daddy would laugh about Ben's big catfish. Ben knew he didn't believe him. It was just a joke between them."

"Yes Ma'am."

Suddenly she remembered why she didn't visit her grandmother more often. A quick visit turned into hours of conversation. Miss Ella was evidently lonely, and a little nosy like her grandmother.

"Miss Ella, do you know of an older black gentleman who lives near-by? He may work taking care of horses."

"Honey, there ain't no colored folks on this road. Where'd you see him?"

"I had a sick horse in my barn a few days ago. He came by and was very helpful. I wanted to thank him."

"He ain't from around here, I can tell you that! He might be a vagrant, Honey. You call the sheriff if he comes back around!"

"Well, I have to go. I love your flowers. They're beautiful!"

"I'll save you some seed. You come back any time. I'm usually here."

Sylvia found out nothing after all the conversation. She wasn't sure where to look for the old man. She laughed at the things Miss. Ella had said. Chuck's warnings hadn't been much different. She did come away with the knowledge that the postman was a bit of a gossip. She'd have to watch what she said to him. Thinking of Mr. Abernathy reminded her of the fence. She'd call later.

Approaching her doorsteps, Sylvia heard someone call to her. She turned to see the two boys, and waved. Cloudy and threatening to rain, it was a good day to make a tuna salad, grab a book, and pile up on the sofa. She emptied the tuna into a bowl, added mayonnaise, then thought of boiled eggs. She left the eggs to cook, and went into the bedroom to change clothes. When she returned to the kitchen she found that the stove was off. Confused, she turned the knob back to the on position.

With salad in hand, Sylvia made her way to the front room. The old sofa was comfortable and the over-stuffed cushions billowed around her as she settled in for the afternoon. Only moments into a classic movie, the telephone rang.

"Hey Sweetie. I'm going shopping for something new to wear. I thought you might like to come along."

"Mom, I'm just being lazy. I'd love to go some other time though. You can come by if you want. I have tuna salad."

"I guess I'll pass. I really need to get this shopping done but I'll call you later."

"Let me know what you buy."

Sylvia was drowsy, and the sound of the raindrops hitting the porch steps was soothing. Enjoying the natural sedative, she soon fell asleep.

Startled by the telephone ringing, she angrily answered. "Hello!"

"What's wrong with you?" asked Chuck

"I'm sorry. I was napping and the phone scared me. How are you?"

"Missin' you. Can I come over or did you want to sleep?"

"No, come on over. I could use the company."

As she hung up the phone, she heard static coming from the television. The picture was gone. She turned off the set and went to dress. Hearing the television from the bathroom, she went back to the front room. It was back on!"

"Okay, this is too weird!" she said aloud

As she turned the set off again, she smelled sweet hay. This time the odor was in the front room, not the kitchen. She tried to remember if she'd ever smelled it anywhere but the kitchen, and remembered that the odor was in the barn. "A barns smell like hay" she whispered to herself. She sat very quiet; listening, smelling, and staring at the blank screen of the television, afraid it would come back on. She was still sitting, brush in hand, when Chuck arrived.

When they walked into the front room the television was once again on. The picture was fine.

"Something weird is going on here. The television went to static and I turned it off. I left the room and it came back on. I turned it off again, sat here watching it, and it stayed off. I went to let you in and now it's on again."

Chuck was laughing, and it was irritating.

"I swear! The stove turned itself off today too. And what about the smell?"

"What smell?"

"It's like sweet hay. I smelled it in the kitchen the day I fainted, and when I was papering the cabinets. It was in here today too. I don't know where it comes from or where it goes!"

"And you mostly smell hay in your kitchen?" he asked smiling

"Except for in the barn and then in here today. I know- the barn would smell like hay."

"No, I bought straw for the barn. There ain't no hay in there."

"Just forget I said anything. It's nothing, I'm sure. You just think it's funny!"

She felt that he was beginning to think she was crazy, like poor old Mrs. Cotton. Perhaps Mrs. Cotton hadn't been so crazy after all, she thought.

"You ain't startin' to believe those stories are you?"

"Just drop it."

"I'm available for round the clock protection."

"Lets change the subject. I'm fine."

After selecting "The Twilight Zone", they settled on the sofa together. Before the show ended she realized that Chuck had gone to sleep. She didn't wake him for a while, but watched him sleep. He looked so much like a little boy. When the show ended, she softly called his name.

"Oh wow I'm sorry! I didn't mean to go to sleep."

"It's all right. I enjoyed watching you sleep."

"You gonna be okay here?"

"I'm fine. Do you need to go?"

"I better."

She walked him to the door and without warning he kissed her. He brushed her hair back from her face and said good night. She said nothing; just watched him walk slowly down the steps.

Chapter Eight

Sylvia was met one morning with the news of Marty deciding to become a veterinarian.

"I'm so happy. You're a natural with the animals and if you've made it through this summer, you'll do fine. What'd your parents say?"

"Anything that'll make me more money than farming is fine with my dad. Mama was pretty happy I finally decided what I want to be."

"It'll be a lot of work, but you can do it. I've got some college books too, so don't go buy anything until you check with me. When will you have to leave?"

"I'm not leaving for two years. I figured I'd take the first two years here, then transfer. I can still work here and go to night classes. You're not rid of me yet!"

"That's great! Some of the classes won't be offered at night, but we'll work around those for you. I'm really proud of you sport."

"Hey you inspired me! I've learned a lot from you this summer."

Sylvia thought back to her summer job. She'd helped the traveling veterinarian make rounds in the county. He had inspired her. Now she had the chance to pass it on to Marty, she thought.

"Dr. Champion?" Mechelle called "Can you take a call on line two?"

"Hello, this is Dr. Champion."

"Yeah, my dogs scratchin' and his hairs fallin' out. I tried the scratch shampoo from the store, but it ain't workin'."

"Can you come in this afternoon?"

"I guess so. Do you want me to bring my dog?"

"Yes Ma'am, I can't treat him without seeing him."

"Can't you give him some shampoo or somethin'?"

"No Ma'am. I need to examine him to see what the problem is. I'll give you back to Mechelle, and she can schedule an appointment."

The telephone went dead.

Mechelle had scheduled two rural customers for late afternoon, so Sylvia was trying to clear the remaining office patients by two o'clock. Just as she was completing her last exam, Mechelle came in.

"Dr. Champion, you'll never believe this!"

"What?"

"That woman who called about her scratching dog? She just called again. The reason she didn't want an appointment was that it's not her dog. Her husbands going bald and someone told her mange shampoo would help! She wanted to know if we'd prescribe a bottle for him!"

"I assume you told her no!"

Marty was laughing.

"Does mange shampoo really work on baldness?"

"Not that I know of. I certainly wouldn't recommend it. You aren't thinking of a way to pay for college are you?" she laughed

"How'd you guess?"

Sylvia was glad Marty would be staying for two more years. He could always read her jokes and bounce them right back.

She left the office, drove two blocks, and remembered she'd left her files.

"Hey, back so soon? That was really quick." Mechelle said

"I forgot my files. Who am I going to see, anyway?"

"The Thompson's on highway four, and Mr. Mack on Clover Lane."

"I'm gone."

High school sweethearts, the Thompsons had been destined to marry. Now ten years into the marriage they were expecting twins, had built a new home, and purchased three cows. Sylvia had known them since grade school. As a favor, she agreed to check the cows for them. After examining the animals, she gave a good report.

"Everything looks fine. I wish I had more time to sit around and catch up on things with you guys, but I have one more call to make. I expect a call when those babies arrive!"

Sylvia drove to Mr. Mack's farm. She didn't particularly like him. His hunting dogs always looked underfed, and lived in confined quarters. He was typically non-social, and had been as far back as she remembered. Mr. Mack approached the dog pens as she gathered her things from the car.

"How are you today, Mr. Mack?"

"You see them clouds? How you think I am? I got plantin' to do and it looks like rain!"

"Mr. Mack, you might consider increasing the dogs food intake. They look a little hungry to me."

"Doc…that's what they call you now ain't it? Them dogs eat all our scraps. They get plenty. I had me one hound was takin' all the others food, but I shot him last week! They ain't sickly are they? I don't want no sick hounds. I need fer um to hunt."

"They seem to be okay. I'll check their records and see when vaccinations are due. You take care. Call if you need us."

She wanted to make an offer to take any unwanted dogs off his hands in the future, but decided it would only spawn more ignorant conversation so she left.

Sylvia thought of her dad while driving back to town. She stopped by the hardware store and found both of her parents still working.

"Mom, Dad, I'm home!" she yelled

"You're crazy girl." her dad replied

"Mom, could you get Matt off my back? He worries me to death about investing. I haven't made enough money to start investing. Where's David?"

"He's on a delivery. He'll go home after that. Did you need to talk to him?"

"I just wanted to say hi."

"Well, you can call him later or come by the house. I wish you and Matt would talk more too. He just tries to help, you know."

"I realize that, Mom, but I don't tell him how to treat his animals just because I'm a vet! I just wish he'd talk about something other than money."

"You'll work it out. If you don't want to invest, just tell him."

"Dad, you look tired. Are you working too hard?"

"You better worry about yourself, little girl. I hear you've been putting in a lot of hours."

"Not too bad right now. Tell David I'll see him later. I'm going on to the house. I love you."

Sylvia noticed a vegetable truck parked at the curb as she left. Squash, onions, tomatoes, and boiled peanuts; the sign said. She made a few purchases and headed home. She was hungry for vegetables. Not the canned variety, but fresh, like Grandma Champion always cooked.

She organized everything necessary in the kitchen, and cooked a vegetable dinner. With everything done, she sat down to eat. The smell again! She continued eating and was aware that it wasn't going away. The possibility of a ghost crossed her mind again. A ghost that smelled of sweet hay! She was amused at the thought. As she ate, she realized that until then, the odor appeared when something unusual happened in the house. Now it appeared for no reason. "I'm analyzing odor behavior!" she laughed to herself.

After dinner she sat at the window looking into the front yard. She remembered that she hadn't called Mr. Abernathy, and reached for the telephone.

"Hi, this is Dr. Champion. I was just checking on the fence."

"I'm finishin' it up now. I'll bring it over on Tuesday afternoon. I think you'll like it. I carved the tops of the pickets."

"I'm sure they look great. I'll be home after five o'clock and can help you dig holes or something."

"Okay. I'll see you then. Oh, you didn't check your box this week. Mails pilin' up in there."

"I'll clean it out right now. Thanks."

"I heard you paid Miss Ella a visit. How'd you like her? Did she say anything about me?"

"She's very nice. I don't remember your name coming up in the conversation, Mr. Abernathy. I'll talk to you later, all right? Good-bye now."

"Bye-bye."

Chapter Nine

Sylvia hadn't seen Chuck in several days. She missed him coming over for dinner and to watch television. Life alone wasn't all she thought it'd be. She loved her house, but it was so quiet in the evenings. There was nothing worth watching on the television, so she went out to the porch. The crickets were chirping, and she could hear a bird singing from his perch on the power line. The porch was her quiet retreat. It was always peaceful there, and the breeze seemed to whisper to her in times of stress or loneliness.

It was late when she went to take her bath. She passed the closet in the hallway and thought of the old note. She hadn't thrown it away, and wasn't sure why. "What was that name?" she mumbled. Mr. Abernathy had called the name, but she couldn't seem to recall. "Squire; Old Squire." she said aloud. Sylvia turned to enter the bathroom and suddenly screamed! The old man from the barn was standing in the hallway. She looked for something to defend herself with, but saw nothing. She reasoned that she needed to remain calm and try not to show any fear. She'd just try to talk to him and get him out of the house, she thought. Then she could call the Sheriff.

"Who are you exactly, and how did you get in my house?"

"I's Ole Squire, Chille. I done met you in dat barn. You call an' I come. Cain't find my Molly, an' cain't leave dis place. Dis me an' Molly's place. Been here long time."

She knew the house had been closed up for years. He wasn't making sense! She noticed that he hadn't changed his clothing since the night in the barn. She wasn't sure of the material. The old coat was thin, and his pants were worn and too short for his height. The lines on his old face seemed at home. He was tall and darker skinned than anyone she'd ever seen. His hands were large and callused. His eyes were dark, and hauntingly sad. Still, he seemed kind, like an old grandfather. She calmed herself and was no longer frightened of him.

"I haven't called anyone Sir. I think you should leave now!"

"I heard you call Ole Squire, an' I come. Done tole you Chille, cain't leave here, jest cain't."

Sylvia couldn't understand what he meant. She knew her doors had been locked and she'd heard no one break a window! She thought of Mrs. Cotton. Perhaps he was a spirit, and the old woman hadn't made up the stories.

"Are you telling me that you're a ghost?"

"Naw, Chille. I ain't said dat."

"You said this place was yours and Molly's. When did you buy this place?"

The old man laughed.

"Slave cain't buy nuttin'. We's had a cabin here. Long gone now doe. Miz Cotton long gone now too."

"You knew Mrs. Cotton?"

"Yep, tried a get rid a me too. I kep telling her cain't go nowhere. Jest cain't."

"I didn't call you that night in the barn. Why'd you come out there?"

"Guess you call on de Lawd. He musta set me in dat barn a hep you."

Sylvia realized that it was the old man who smelled of sweet hay. He'd said he tended horses. That would explain the odor, but she couldn't accept that he was a ghost. Here stood a man who looked quite ordinary, but claimed to be a slave. She knew it was impossible.

"Squire, can anyone see you? I mean if people come to my house they can see you too, right?"

"Naw. Me an' Miz Cotton, we try dat. She say "Ole Squire, dis Miz Martin." Dat woman look rite through me. I try talkin' other fokes too. Did'n work."

Sylvia was disappointed. How would anyone believe her? Without being able to show them, she knew they wouldn't.

"So you say that God put you in the barn, and you're in here because I called out your name?"

"Dat rite. Awmighty knowed I hep hawses. Cain't touch um doe. Cain't do much a nuttin'. Jest be here. Some thangs I do. Dat box wid fokes in it? Ole Squire made it go way."

"My television! You really scared me that night. What about the knocking, and in the kitchen when I fainted? Did you wipe my face?"

"Wipe it wid dis rag."

He pulled an old faded cloth from his pocket.

"Lawd let me hep fokes, but jest if he say. Cain't work wid des hands no moe. I's feel bad a scarin' you. Don't know bout no knockin'. Gots me some big feets. Might be Ole Squire walkin' roun'."

"Did you turn off the stove?"

"Yep, gone catch fire. No body watchin'."

"When did you die?"

"Don't reckon I's dead, Chille. I'd be gone a glory if I's dead! You thank Ole Squire dead?"

She didn't know what to say. He had to realize that things had changed. He said he couldn't do anything!

"Are you hungry?"

"Don't eat. Don't sleep no moe neither. Jest calls Molly. Figure dey sent her get sompin'. She be back. Dey won't send her far."

"If you're still living, why wouldn't you get hungry?"

"I figure Awmighty want Ole Squire rest now. He fix it so's I don't get hungry, don't works no moe. Jest stays here waitin' fo' Molly. Reckon he done seen how hard I work afo'."

The old man laughed as if he'd thought of something funny.

"Wait'll my Molly see me! She gone be proud I ain't workin' so hard. She ustah cry bout des hands. She rub um an' jest cry."

Sylvia was overwhelmed. Her logical side told her that this couldn't be. She and her brother had laughed at their grandmother's tales of spirits. She told the man that she needed to get some sleep and he was gone; vanished into thin air! As she lay awake, she wondered if he could see everything she did. She was unnerved at the idea. It would be impossible for her to sleep. After drinking a cup of hot chocolate, she decided to find out if she could actually summon the old man by calling out his name.

"Squire"

"Yeah Chille."

She'd done it! He was a spirit. A slave spirit; living in her home. Of all the houses available, she'd chosen the one with a ghost! She reasoned that perhaps by convincing him he was deceased, he would leave and go on to "glory" as he called it.

"Squire, do you know that this year is nineteen sixty-four? There've been no slaves since the civil war. That was over one hundred years ago! That would make you well over one hundred years old. You couldn't have lived that long you know."

"Chille, nobody ever read you outta dat good book did dey? Miz Amy read us outta dat book bout a man live nine hundred years old. I figure Ole Squire got plenty time left."

"Who was Miss Amy?"

He explained that she'd been the Masters youngest child. She'd been concerned for the slave children and secretly taught many of them to read. She read to the slaves from the bible on Sunday afternoons.

"We all sat on de groun' by de big oak tree an' we listen reel good. Miz Amy wus a good chille; treat us nice."

"Did you have a pretty good life Squire?"

"Ain't no good life fo' no slave, Chille. Hard work, long days, straw beds, an' dirt floors. Chillins sold off if Massa's a mind a sell um. Thangs better now doe."

"They sold your children?"

"Not mine. Me an' Molly buried two chillins, raise up two. I's sold off from my mama doe. All of us wus cept one brother. Fokes say he wus Massa's baby. He stay wid Mama."

"Did you see your brothers after they sent you away?"

"Naw Chille. We's all sold different massas. Never did see Mama affah dey took us way neither. We rode a wagon to da sellin' place. One my brothers, he cry all way deah. Mama done tole us boys "Don't ya'll cry none. Stand up tall! Might get same massa." Didn't doe. All went different way."

"Where are your children?"

"Left affah de war. Miz Amy learnt um a read an' write. Dey working up nawth. Molly pack um some food when dey left. She wave to um far as she could see um."

"It must've been hard on Molly."

"Hard, but we knows dey gone do good."

"You never saw them again?"

"Naw, never did."

By the time the conversation ended, Sylvia was in tears. She tried to imagine being sold off from her mother as a child. She didn't understand how anyone could have allowed it to happen. Those who purchased children had mothers of their own, she thought. Why didn't they think of how their own mother's would've felt? After hearing his story, she decided she could share her home with the old man until she could find a way to help him leave.

Chapter Ten

The new veterinarian's reputation grew over the next few months. Business was so good that Sylvia hardly had time for anything. Most of her hours away from work were spent resting, or talking with Old Squire. She grew closer to him, like an endearing friend. She'd listen to his stories about Molly, and wish she could give him what he most wanted. Conversations were mostly kept light to avoid bringing up the slavery issue. Those stories were hard for Sylvia to hear.

Chuck wasn't in the picture as much as before. She did think of him every day and wanted a relationship, but hadn't found it so important to make sacrifices. He hadn't expressed any desire to move the relationship further either. So it was "see you when I can" for both of them.

One afternoon Sylvia came into the house crying. She felt that everything was passing her by, and she called to her friend.

"What wrong, Chille?"

"I don't have a life! I never see my family and I'm worried about my little brother being drafted. On top of everything else, I don't have any time for Chuck!"

"Chuck a good man, I thanks. You gone marry wid em?"

"I don't have time for a commitment, Squire."

"You need somebody take care a you."

She laughed. Often, she forgot from whence he came.

"The world has changed. Women work now, and we enjoy it. I don't want anyone to take care of me! When I marry, it'll be for love and nothing else!"

"You a strange Chille. My Molly work too. Did'n have no say bout it doe. Massa wife did'n work. She had fine clothes, an' he took good care a her. I want my Molly have fine clothes an' sit up in a soft chair. Never did give her dat doe. Could'n' do nuttin' cept what I's tole to. Man auttah take care a his wife if he want. Me an' Molly ustah laugh bout it. I sit her down on a crate box an' wrap a burlap piece roun' her shoulders like it wus a fine shawl. She awder tea an' cakes, jest like Massa wife. It wus funny. You jest should'a seen it Chille."

It wasn't funny. It was the saddest thing she'd ever heard a man tell about his wife. Somehow, listening to Squire always put her back on track. How could she complain about her life after hearing his stories? She was inspired to make time for loved ones.

The next Sunday, Sylvia cooked everything on page eleven of "Women's Helper" magazine. She'd never prepared a meal for her family and was proud that everything was going so well. The vegetable casserole browned beautifully, and the mushroom-coated roast was perfection. The guest arrived right on time.

"Mom, come see if I've forgotten anything."

"Everything looks wonderful! You've become quite the cook."

"Hey, can we watch the football game?" her dad called out

"No, we're ready to eat dinner."

During dinner, Sylvia noticed that David was unusually quiet.

"What's wrong with you? You're way too quiet. Where's the snide remark about my cooking?"

"Everything taste great, Sis."

"You feeling okay? This was a prime opportunity for you and your aggravating jokes."

"I didn't want to spoil the gathering, but I've been called up by the draft."

"Want more tea, Dad? Try the rolls, they're really good."

"Hey, did you hear me Sis?"

She ran from the room crying. What did he know about fighting and killing? He'd never even hunted with his friends! Why couldn't the fighting just stop? she wondered

"Sylvia, Honey I know. We all went through this yesterday. Your brother is okay with this, and we have to be strong for him. It was so hard for him to tell you. Go and talk to him, all right?"

"I'm sorry, Mom. I didn't mean to react so badly, but it was a shock. I've expected it, but I guess I didn't realize how bad it would hit me when it happened."

She wiped her eyes, hugged her mom, and went back to the kitchen.

"Leave it to you to screw up a party!" she laughed

"You okay, Sis?"

"Hey, if you are…then I am. We'll write lots of letters while you're away. I'll visit your friends and send newspapers to keep you updated on local events. You'll be back in no time."

David pushed his chair back from the table, and offered his sister a much-needed hug. He promised to call with details of his departure date so that she could plan time to spend with him.

Later, with everyone gone, Sylvia cried until she cried out. David had seemed to be accepting being drafted. She knew she'd have to be strong for him. After that night, she would try. Perhaps when the visions in her head disappeared, visions of the mischievous little boy who always hid her favorite doll, who proudly wore the Superman cape she'd bought for his fifth birthday, and who constantly reminded her that he was the baby of the family. Maybe, if those images left, she could be strong.

Chapter Eleven

The first year in the new clinic had passed quickly. Sylvia's workload was more than she could handle alone. Mechelle requested applications from the next graduating class of Auburn. After only one week, she'd received ten replies. Interviews were scheduled, and Sylvia chose a new partner, Richard Lane.

Dr. Lane was a pleasant addition. He was bright, ruggedly handsome, and his sense of humor kept the staff competing for best joke of the day. Marty and Mechelle had worked out so well at the clinic, and with each other. It seemed too much to hope for that a forth person would blend in. Richard was the exception.

Sylvia had more personal time after adding a partner. She and Chuck were seeing more of each other, and she spent as much time as possible with David before he left for boot camp. One afternoon she'd taken David to the old ferry landing. They fished, and skipped rocks across the rippling water. Most of the afternoon was spent just reflecting on childhood memories.

"Hey Sis" he'd said "I want to remember us right here at this spot, while I'm over there."

"It's been a good place for us to come when we wanted to escape the world, huh?"

"Or Dad!"

"Remember the time you broke Mom's vase and we thought you'd surely get killed for it? I ran away with you and we hid out down here."

"Yeah, I remember. We weren't too creative. Mom and Dad knew this was our favorite place and found us within the hour. Why did you go with me?"

"You threatened to beat me up if I didn't!"

"I don't remember that part! I just thought you were worried about me."

With David gone, she often thought of that last afternoon. It was if she'd frozen the moment forever and could see his face each time she remembered. Her dad refused to hire someone to fill David's position at the hardware store, and her mom was there much more, running things while he made deliveries. Sylvia wondered how many lives had changed because of the war.

Everyone at the clinic kept Sylvia's spirits up during that time. They were all young and enthusiastic. She noticed that Richard and Mechelle were often taking breaks together, and thought there might be some flirtation being shared. Mechelle mentioned that she might ask Richard to a family reunion celebration.

"What do you think he'd say?"

"I'm not sure. Those occasions are sort of personal, aren't they? I guess if people are seriously dating, they might ask each other. Are you seriously interested in Richard?"

"I don't know! I just thought since he's not from here and don't go out much, he might enjoy it. He might meet some nice people."

"Don't listen to me. You're sweet to think of him. I'll bet he'll accept your invitation."

Later that week, Mechelle did ask, and Richard accepted. Sylvia had been right about their flirtation. That first date grew into a relationship.

Marty wasn't involved with anyone. He would joke with Sylvia that the two of them were too dedicated to their work to settle down with anyone. Everyone working at the clinic became close. They were Sylvia's extended family. She did want more in her life one day, but wasn't sure Chuck would be the one. At times she did picture how their children would look if they married, and how they'd look when they grew old. Those pictures didn't appear often, however. She was in no hurry to change her life.

Chapter Twelve

Chuck stopped by the clinic on a Friday afternoon. Sylvia hadn't expected him.

"I'm surprised to see you here. Is anything wrong?"

"No, I couldn't get you off my mind. Let's go somewhere special tonight. I'll pick you up at seven. Dress casual."

"Casual? I thought you said special."

"It'll be special, just not too fancy. See you tonight."

Mechelle heard the conversation and found it mysteriously romantic.

"What if he's going to propose or something? Don't you just love surprises?"

"I'd prefer to know what he's up to! I don't think it would be a proposal."

For the rest of the day Sylvia thought of what Mechelle had said. She hadn't even thought in terms of marriage, but she did believe that she loved Chuck. He arrived promptly at seven o'clock with roses. She wondered if maybe it was a step toward a more serious commitment, if perhaps Mechelle was right.

"Okay, what's up? I hate surprises."

"Don't you trust me?"

They drove to somewhere near Augusta, and Chuck offered no information. Suddenly, he turned into a dirt drive leading to an open field. There were bleachers and floodlights set up. She spotted the stage.

"An outdoor concert!"

"This okay with you?"

"It's great! I haven't been to one of these since college."

They sat for hours listening to the different artist. Occasionally, Chuck held her hand, and leaned over to kiss her several times during the night. It was magical. Sylvia was convinced that the relationship was changing.

When the music ended, it was nearly one o'clock. Chuck suggested that they pick up something to eat and get a room for the night.

"It's a long drive back."

"I guess it would be okay."

She was nervous as they pulled into the motel. She'd known him for quite a long time and felt that she was in love with him. Still, she was hesitant to make this step. Most of her college friends had found her very reserved. She'd dated one boy, who she thought she cared deeply for. It didn't end well. She promised herself that she wouldn't be intimate with anyone again without love and commitment. She needed to know exactly where she stood with Chuck.

"I think we need to talk before we get out."

"Okay. What about?"

"Us! I need to know what this means. I know how I feel, but I'm not sure how you feel."

"And how do you feel?"

"I've fallen in love with you. You must know that!"

"Hey, that's pretty heavy! I don't know what to say. Are we stayin' or not?"

That was it. He offered nothing of his feelings. She felt humiliated that she'd shared her feelings.

"I want to go home!"

"What's your problem? You're actin' like some little fourteen year-old! Man did I have you figured all wrong. Why can't things just be fun? Whatever happens; happens. How come you gotta make a big deal out of it! Did you think I spent all this time on you for nothin'? Wasted time!"

Sylvia fought back tears, and said nothing. The drive to her house was silent. She wanted to take back what she'd said about loving him, but it was out there and she couldn't take it back. When they reached her house, she quickly left the truck. She heard him pull away as she approached the steps. She didn't look back.

Facing Mechelle would be hard the next day. The poor girl had actually expected an engagement announcement.

Sylvia thought of Squire and realized how difficult it would have been to explain him anyway. Chuck would never have agreed to live with a ghost, and Sylvia wouldn't leave Squire. She felt that she'd been led to that house to find him and see him on his way. Thinking in those terms helped her accept what had happened. "It couldn't have worked anyway", she said

"Squire?"

"Yeah Chille."

"I'm going to help you find your Molly. I promise. You're a good friend to me, you know."

"You thanks you gone fine her?"

"We'll find her somehow."

Exhausted, Sylvia went to bed and slept until noon the next day. She called Richard and offered him a week off to visit his family. She needed the extra work to clear her mind. If she kept busy, she wouldn't think of Chuck.

It was a beautiful day outside, and she thought it a good day to plant the seeds Miss Ella had sent over. She planted those in front of the porch, and morning glory seeds by the fence. They'd be colorful vines before long, she imagined. When the last seed was covered with soil, Sylvia went inside. She thought of David. She hadn't written in several days. She knew he expected her letters. She grabbed her pad and pen, and went out to the porch to write.

"Squire?"

"I's here."

"I planted all the seeds today. We'll have some nice flowers soon."

"Dats nice. It bout six o'clock."

"Six o'clock?"

She thought of her clock in the front room. The repairman had found nothing wrong, but after bringing it home, it went back to six o'clock.

"Are you changing the time on my clock?"

"Clock cain't get pass six."

"Why not?"

"Molly never ded come in pass six. Long as it ain't pass six, she ain't late."

She thought of her promise to find Molly.

"Squire, where were the slaves buried on this place."

He tried to explain that everything had changed. The land was split up and he wasn't sure anymore. He gave her directions, using the boundaries he could remember. She rode up the highway, turned right then rode down another. She lost site of any evidence that a plantation was ever there. She returned home. She was hopeful that the local courthouse held records which could help.

The day ended, and she was surprised to find herself not overly depressed. Realizing that she'd made a bad choice wasn't so hard. Chuck had appeared arrogant in the beginning. His personality after then had been an act. The act ended, and he became himself again. She wouldn't easily trust men in the future, but knew she'd be okay.

Sylvia awoke the next morning with a new idea.

"Squire."

"I hears ya."

"Come with me. We're going to search for the old cemetery."

"What you wanta see dat fo'?"

"I'm just curious. I like old cemeteries and I'd like to know where the slaves were buried."

"Ole Squire cain't leave dis place. Done tole you dat. Cain't go pass dat road."

"Just get in the car!"

"Cain't get in no car neither."

"Well, stand on the bumper, then."

"Yes Ma'am, but it ain't gone work."

She backed the car out into the highway. She turned to see that Squire was back on the porch. She parked the car and laughed.

"Tole you. You don't listen reel good! Don't know why you want go where dead fokes is noway."

She felt sure someone had stumbled across the old graves in the area. She'd search the courthouse when she had time, and ask some of the older hunters in town.

Chapter Thirteen

The next week, Sylvia threw herself into her work: surgeries, regular and rural patients, and emergencies. By the end of the week, she'd worked through any depression she'd felt. Everyone noticed the change and was glad to have the old Dr. Champion back. When Dr. Lane returned the following Monday, she took a couple of days off.

Old Squire had asked each day if Sylvia had found Molly. She knew she shouldn't have promised to find her. She stopped by the courthouse on Tuesday and requested information. The clerk asked what name the land was deeded to during the time period requested. Sylvia realized she'd never asked Old Squire who owned the land. She went home to talk with him.

She made a glass of tea, and called her friend. He appeared, and looked around the room as if expecting to see Molly.

"She isn't here Squire. I'm trying to locate some record of burials on this land. If we can find proof that Molly died, I think you'll be free to join her."

"You done say you fine my Molly! You promise you would. Now you telling me my Molly dead? Molly ain't dead! Dats bout de meanest one thang anybody ever tole Ole Squire. Me an' Molly talk bout goin a glory. Molly ain't done gone a glory widout me. Don't you call me no moe! Don't speaks my name!"

"Squire? Please don't go away. I'm sorry!"

It was no use. He wouldn't answer. For days she called, but he wouldn't show his face. She had hurt him worse than all that had been done to him in the past. She knew he was still in the house. She smelled the hay and occasionally heard him knocking. She finally stopped calling.

Sylvia researched the property back to the Cotton's purchase. There was a partial record showing purchase date, and their names. The name of the previous owner wasn't listed, and the adjoining page was missing. She couldn't search any further without the names.

She wanted to tell someone about Squire. It hadn't been so bad when he was there to talk to her. Now that he was gone, she just wanted to talk about him and his life. Remembering how everyone treated Mrs. Cotton, she put the idea away.

Life went on for Sylvia. Her work with the animals had become well known. Plans to open a zoo near Athens were discussed, and she was asked to be a consultant on the project. She hadn't dealt with wild animals other than an occasional squirrel or bird, but she accepted. She talked with a friend who'd taken a position with the Atlanta zoo. He offered tutoring help when necessary.

It'd been two months since Old Squire disappeared. Sylvia would often sit in the swing and think of their conversations. One evening, she sat on the swing and told him of her new position with the zoo. He didn't answer.

"Squire, if I could give you what you need, I swear I would. If what I said hurt you, I'm sorry. You know that Molly must be gone by now. She couldn't still be walking around here lost. She would've come home by now! I'll leave you alone and not talk to you anymore."

There was only silence. She'd hoped to shake him up and make him appear. She knew he enjoyed the talks, although they were usually about Molly. She'd keep her word, and not speak to him again. He'd have to come to her.

Chapter Fourteen

David had been gone for nine months. Each month had been agony for Sylvia and her family. Soon he'd be home. She'd written faithfully. Some days finding something new to write about had been difficult, but she knew sending something was important.

It was a Tuesday, in November. Sylvia returned from an emergency call and was locking up the clinic when the telephone rang.

"Sylvia?"

"Hey Daddy. How are you?"

"Honey, you need to come to the house as soon as possible."

"What is it?"

"Just drive carefully. We'll see you in a few minutes."

She knew. She was sure it was David. She pulled into the driveway of her parent's home and could see the neighbors, Jeremy and Lisa, standing with Mr. Thornton from the bank. The preacher was talking with them. She stared at the open doorway of the house, not wanting to get out of her car. David's best friend Brad walked slowly toward the car. He reached for the door handle, and she quickly pushed the lock. She turned up the volume of the radio, and looked away. He walked back to the house to get her father.

"Sylvia, open the door honey!"

She stared out the passenger window as if everything would be okay if she just didn't get out of the car.

"Honey, please turn off the engine and open the door! Your mother needs you inside."

She sat for another moment then opened the door. The engine was still running and the radio blaring. Her dad pulled her from the car, and she collapsed in his arms. Brad turned off the engine, silencing the radio.

"Daddy, I can't do this!" she cried

"I know Baby. Let's just get into the house."

"Where's Matt, Daddy? Matt should be here."

"He's on the way, Baby."

Sylvia found her mother sitting quietly at the dining room table. She was looking through the family picture album, eyes fixed on one particular photograph.

"Mom, let's put that away for now."

"Look at this picture, Sylvia. Do you remember those terrible striped pants? He just cried and cried until I bought them. I never understood why he wanted them so badly, but they were awful, weren't they?"

"I remember. How old is he there?"

"About four. It's funny that no matter how old you children get, I still see you as three or four in my mind. I enjoyed those years so much."

"Mom, please. Let's go in the kitchen. I'll make us some coffee or a glass of tea or whatever you want. I don't want to look at those pictures anymore Mom!"

Sylvia pulled her mother from the chair, and held her tightly.

"I have to be strong for your Daddy. He's having a real hard time. I'm worried about his health. Is that Matt? I heard a car out back."

That Tuesday in November would forever be a worst day in Sylvia's life. Nothing would ever compare, not even the day of the funeral. It was the initial shock, the severe blinding pain of that Tuesday, in November, which would never go away.

Somehow, the funeral did take place a few days later. Full military honors; Taps, twenty-one-gun salute, and a flag. The government's payment-in-full for one brother's life. "Not enough. Not nearly enough!" Sylvia had said. She would remain angry throughout her life about David's death.

Late in the afternoon, Sylvia asked Matt to take a ride with her. She stopped by for flowers, and drove to the ferry landing. Matt didn't question, he was just there for support.

"Gosh, I remember this place Sis."

"David and I came here just before he left. Do you believe we can come back after we die?"

"Oh, I don't know. I'd rather not think about it."

"If David could still be anywhere on earth, I'll bet he'd be right here. Don't you think?"

He didn't answer. He watched as she walked to the waters edge. She carefully separated the flowers, and tossed them one at a time into the water. She stood watching as they floated downstream, dancing on the ripples. Matt was silent. He wasn't sure what to say. He was just handling the situation the best that he could for himself.

The kids at the clinic were somber when Sylvia returned to work. Work had always been her way of dealing with any problems. She'd spent as much time as she could stand with her family. They were hurting every bit as much, and it seemed worse to share the pain over and over. Being back to work, she could concentrate on other things.

She wasn't hungry when she reached home that evening. She drank some juice and checked her mail, which had piled up with her away. Halfway through the stack of junk mail, utility bills, and insurance advertisements, she spotted a letter from David. She just sat on the porch swing clutching the letter and crying. She couldn't bring herself to open the envelope. She drew her knees under her chin and screamed…David!! When she looked up, Old Squire was standing by the porch steps.

"Old Squire! I'm so glad you've come back. My brother was killed in the war. He's never coming back and I don't know how to deal with it. Please don't go away. I don't want to be alone."

"I sorry bout yo' brother. It hurt when ya knows you never gone see somebody agin'."

"I'm sorry for what I said to you, Squire. I realize now, how you must feel. You believe that Molly is coming home if you want. That belief has kept you going all these years."

"Squire knows Molly ain't comin'. You's rite. She done gone an' lef Ole Squire."

"I still believe that you'll see her again in glory, just like I'll see my brother. We just have to find a way to get you there!"

"I bleeves ya, Chille. If any person can get me there, you can. I jest knows it! I ain't gone be mad wid ya no moe. I's yo' frien agin'."

"What made you come back?"

"I hears yo' cryin', like you's dyin' or sompin'. Cain't stands no cryin' like dat."

Old Squire noticed the crumpled envelope in her hand.

"What ya got in dat paper?"

"It's a letter from David. I guess the mail took longer to get here than he did."

"You gone read it? Might be impodent. Bet it de lass thang he wrote an' he wrote it a you."

"I can't. I'm afraid he might have been scared near the end. He might have felt that he was in danger."

"You do what bes' fo' you. Put it way. You jest might read it one day. Might read it a Ole Squire!"

Sylvia didn't open that letter. She put it away in a box on the top shelf of her closet. She didn't discuss the letter with anyone but Squire, afraid that the family might want it opened.

Glad to have Squire back in her life, she was more determined than ever to help him. It would be hard to let him go if she could find a way, but knew that it would be the right thing. She imagined he would be different after he knew Molly wasn't coming home. So much of his conversations had been about where Molly might be, or when Molly would be home.

Chapter Fifteen

It was hard to believe that two years had passed. Marty was going off to Auburn. He promised to call often and ask for answers to the major exams.

Mechelle agreed to fill in as assistant for a while. She would be leaving as soon as she could establish herself with an accounting firm. So many changes had taken place. Losing Marty was hard, and Sylvia didn't know how she'd manage when Mechelle left.

Richard and Mechelle announced their engagement one morning. Sylvia had expected them to eventually make the decision, and was happy for them.

"When and where do we plan the wedding?"

"Oh, not till next year. I want to finish school and get established." Mechelle answered

Richard was beaming with pride as he extended Mechelle's hand for Sylvia's approval.

"Not too shabby! Now lets see some patients. We still have work to do around here!"

Sylvia was envious of the couple. She watched as they admired everything each other did. She was sure that they'd have children. The boys would inherit Richard's jaw line, and the girls would have Mechelle's eyes. She was daydreaming of the wedding when Mechelle asked her to pick up on line two.

"Hello, Dr. Champion here."

"Real impressive, Sis! I've never heard you referred to as Doctor."

It was Matt. He'd been calling more often since David's death. She felt that he believed she loved David more, and was trying to bridge the gap between them.

"How are the kids?"

"That's why I'm calling. Stephanie wants to come and spend a week with you. School is out, and we could bring her down this weekend, if it's okay."

"I'd love it! Doesn't Jonathan want to come?"

"He has camp with the church, and all of his friends are going. It's a guy thing."

"Well, I'll see ya'll this weekend. Thanks for letting her come."

Sylvia was excited. Not sure what a twelve year old would enjoy, she consulted Mechelle.

"Oh, be prepared to stay up all night listening to music, talking about boys and crushes, and buy plenty of junk food. You know, chips, dip, cookies, soda."

"My brother would kill me!"

"Hey, that's what aunts are for. I'm sure she's excited to get away from the parents and stay with the cool younger aunt."

"I'll need a crash course in cool!"

Sylvia was busy for the next two days. When she closed the clinic, she hit the stores. She bought enough snacks to feed the town, new albums, matching sleep shirts, and a princess phone for Stephanie's room. This would be the most fun she'd had since college, she thought.

She told Old Squire of the expected guest. He was very excited.

"Ain't been no chillins here since Miz Cotton's boy. He's a good little boy, sho' wus."

"You never mentioned a child living here. Did he ever see you?"

"Yeah, Chille. I's watch em since he boan, till de day he get hurt. He seen me dat day. Dat wus first day his mama seen Ole Squire too. Dat boy up in de oak tree. He fall down to de groun'. Lawd set me under dat tree a pick em up. Toted em to his mama. Scared her near bout dead, Negro carryin' her boy. He did'n live much affah dat. Live long nuff a tell his mama I hep em doe. Miz Cotton cry an' cry when dat boy die. We's friens' affah den."

"That's terrible! Did they have other children?"

"Naw, jest dat boy."

Sylvia wondered if her niece would see or hear Old Squire. She feared that the child would be frightened if she thought a ghost lived in the house. She would talk to Squire before Stephanie arrived. She didn't want to offend him, but would need for him to be quiet and stay out of sight.

She thought of the Cotton child and wondered where he'd been buried. It occurred to her that she might have many bodies on her land! The Cotton family had built the house in the thirties, so she hoped the child had been placed in a cemetery in town.

Stephanie arrived on Friday. Her dad dropped her off at the clinic. She was fascinated with the animals, especially a raccoon in the back room.

"He was trapped by a farmer. They carry rabies and can be dangerous! He isn't tame, Stephanie." Sylvia warned

The child walked through the clinic and looked at all of the client photographs on the wall. She wanted to help with the shampoos.

"I wash our dogs at home. I can do a good job!"

"You may help Mechelle, but let her tell you which dogs are biters."

"I'm not scared of dogs! They don't ever bite me."

"Go and talk to Mechelle please."

She was so inquisitive. She wanted to know how every instrument was used, what each medication cured, and why anyone would cut on a poor animal just to keep them from having babies. Sylvia worried that she'd go home with more knowledge than her parents would've wanted.

The afternoon went well. After only three hours, Stephanie was convinced that she could handle her aunt's job.

"This is fun. Tomorrow, can I give shots or some pills to the animals?"

"You're making my job look too easy! I think helping to bathe the dogs will be enough for now."

The girls headed home after work. Sylvia suggested a movie, later.

"I love to go to the movies. Dad won't let me go much though. He thinks I might see something bad!"

"We'll screen the previews before we go. I don't think the downtown cinema has anything suggestive."

"Oh darn!"

She found the child to be delightfully intelligent, and they became close that week. Each night they sat up watching television, and would laugh at the really bad dialogue in the old movies. By the end of the week, Stephanie didn't want to leave. Before she left, they agreed to spend every summer together.

With Stephanie gone, the house was quiet. Sylvia was glad that her niece hadn't seen or heard Old Squire. It would've been more than she could explain to the twelve year old. She missed talking with her friend.

"Hey Squire"

He appeared across the room.

"I's reel quiet like you say. Dat girl reel nice. Reel nice Chille."

"Yes she is. She went home today. I'll miss her being around."

"You got Ole Squire."

"I sure do. I don't know what I'd do without you here."

Sylvia remembered that she needed names for her research. She hadn't been back to the courthouse since he reappeared.

"Squire, who was the owner of the plantation here?"

"Massa Kinsey, den Massa Kinsey."

"The same Kinsey's that the town is named after?"

"Guess so. Don't know bout dat."

"What did you mean Master Kinsey then Master Kinsey?"

"Ole Massa die an' de plantation wus split up. I stay on wid young Massa Kinsey."

Dats where I mets my Molly. She come stay on young Massa James Kinsey land."

"How old were you when old Master Kinsey died?"

"Don't know. Not no full growed man. Still did my shara work doe. Massa James Kinsey one what made me haws keeper. Why I's had me ten hawses an' six mules a see affah. Better an' field work. Dats fo' sho'."

"Miss Amy, was she young or old Master Kinsey's daughter?"

"She young Massa chille. He had two boys an' Miz Amy."

"Who were the boys?"

"Let me thanks. Seem like one dem boys be James, an' one wus Sam."

"Do you remember the war? Where did you go after you were freed. You were freed weren't you?"

"Yeah, Chille. I seen dat war. Some fokes got burn rite out, but we made it. Got me a paper says I free man. Keeps it wid me all de time."

Squire pulled a paper from his pocket and showed it to her. She carefully studied the old writing, finding it hard to believe that she was reading a freedom paper from so long ago.

"Wes stay here. Massa let us stay in de cabin fo' Molly working in de big house an' me tendin' hawses."

"Were you paid wages?"

"Don't know bout no wages. Now an' den, Massa give me some coins. I save um up a buy Molly sompin."

"What'd you buy?"

"I seen dis rang in a book what Miz Amy had. Miz Amy taked my coins, an' she awder it fo' me. Molly cry when she seen it. Would'n' never wear it doe; scared a losin' it. Put it in a tin box. Some slaves jest turn out. We heard bout dey Massas runnin' um off. Some jest run off on dey own. We did'n have no place a go, an' we watton beat like some we heard bout, so we's stay. Growed some food rite out deah. Massa give us some seed. I's gone grow some cotton or bacca. Gone sell it! Massa would'n' have dat doe. Say no body gone buy from no Negro, noway."

Sylvia was engulfed by visions of Squire's life. She could feel every emotion he expressed in his unpolished language. She tried to imagine her dad living as Squire had lived. To be told that you weren't allowed to prosper, not even able to have hope of providing better for your family, was unimaginable. She thought of how much she'd paid contractors to remodel her house, men who used their skill and were paid for their skill. Old Squire had used up his body, soul, and skills working for nothing. He'd said he hadn't been beaten, but he had been. Maybe not with a whip, but beaten just the same. To take away a man's pride and rob him of his dignity in the presence of his family was to beat a man in the worse way.

"I'm sorry Squire. It must be horrible for you to remember those times."

"Chille, dere you goes talking like Ole Squire never did have no hope. Hope kep' me goin'. We gather up an' singed bout hope. Don't you worry bout Ole Squire. Wait'll Molly see me. She gone be proud I not be working so hard no moe."

Chapter Sixteen

Sylvia would think of her conversation with Squire, between patients the next day. She couldn't shake the sorrow she felt for him. She wanted so badly to give him his freedom. She went back to the courthouse.

The assistant file clerk, Miss Abbott, recognized her from her last visit.

"Hi, did you find more information?"

"Yes. The land was the Kinsey Plantation before the war. I'm not sure how long after then."

Miss Abbott pulled several books from the shelves. She found an old Will, and a reference of land purchase. Sylvia obtained copies of both, and sat down to read. The Will dated eighteen hundred five, contained several slaves. The slave left to James, was Old Squire. She was shocked as she read how each child had inherited a feather bed, an animal, and one slave. The slaves had been given as property along with the cattle, horses, and land. The Will was signed, James Kinsey. He must have been old Master Kinsey. The son would have been young Master Kinsey, she assumed.

Old Squire had mentioned that he wasn't fully grown when the old man died. That would've been somewhere near eighteen hundred five. If he were a teen, by the war he would've been in his seventies. She searched later records and found boundaries for the land. The early English writing was difficult to read.

"You might check library records." Miss Abbott suggested

The library had some information on local cemeteries, and the librarian offered the number of a local historian. After returning home, Sylvia called.

"I'm seeking information on the old Kinsey Plantation and any graves which might have been marked when found."

"Oh, the Kinsey graves were relocated several years ago, when the river was re-routed. Some were moved to a church west of town."

"Do you know of any slave graves found?"

"No. It's sad but many of the slave graves weren't marked back then, or only marked with rocks. I have no record of the Kinsey slave graves."

Sylvia returned home feeling that everything was lost. She'd hoped to find a grave. At least then, she could've told Squire where Molly rested. Now she realized that Molly might be forever under the river. She thought of her grandmother Champion, and her stories of spirits. She thought perhaps she could learn something from her.

Driving over to her grandmother's, Sylvia felt guilty. She never visited and hadn't even called since David's funeral. She parked in the front yard and walked to the door.

"Grandma?"

"That you, Sylvia?"

"Yes Ma'am, let me in. The screens hooked."

After listening to her grandmother talk for an hour, Sylvia brought up the subject of spirits.

"You know those ghost stories you told when we were little?"

"Yeah, those were told to me by my daddy. They were true, you know."

"Did he ever say why a ghost would be in a house or how to get them to leave?"

"He said sometimes folks get trapped, and can't find their way. Sometimes they have unfinished business, or died by murder and need to let someone know who killed them.

I don't think he ever said how to get them out of the house. If he did, I don't recall it. I remember how to make one appear in the flesh, though. He said, if you say "What in the name of God is thy will with me", they'll appear. I wouldn't ever say it if I thought there was one. I don't want to see no ghost!"

Sylvia could see it was a dead end. It made sense that he might be trapped, or had unfinished business the day he died, but she didn't think he'd been murdered. He didn't even believe he was dead! Discussing it with him would do no good. He knew that Molly was dead, and that didn't free him, so he wasn't trapped just waiting for her.

"How come you're interested in those stories now? You and David used to laugh at me when I told them. You didn't believe me back then. I miss David, don't you?"

"Yes Ma'am, I'll always miss him. He shouldn't have been over there...shouldn't have died. About the spirits, I just thought about the stories and never remembered hearing why they were in anyone's houses. I really need to go. I'll see you soon, I promise." she said as she walked to the door.

At home, she asked Squire more questions about his past. She hoped to find an answer as to why he'd been left behind.

"Do you remember the last time you saw the big house?"

"Yep. It wus moanin' of de big storm. Everythang gone affah dat storm. I waked up on de groun'. I call Molly an' call Molly. Never did see her; did'n' see nobody."

Sylvia reasoned that it must have been a tornado. She wondered how many more died that day. She thought perhaps she might find an old newspaper record of the storm.

"What year was it, Squire?"

"Don't know dat. Affah de war. Affah I gots my paper."

She had wondered why Squire hadn't found it strange that the scenery had changed. The storm would explain that. He said everything had been destroyed.

Sylvia would once again put the mystery aside. She had to concentrate on work and the zoo project. Construction was under way and she had received notice to appear in Athens for a meeting.

Chapter Seventeen

The lobby was filled with barking dogs when Sylvia arrived at the clinic. A poor cat was hiding under the corner sofa, and pet owners were frantically trying to call off their dogs.

"Mechelle! Get some of these animals into exam rooms please!"

"Okay, Dr. Champion. We've been waiting for you!"

"Where's Dr. Lane?"

"He'll be a little late this morning."

"Great!"

It took until one o'clock for Sylvia to catch up with exams. Richard hadn't arrived until twelve. She was furious, but managed to remain quiet until the clients left. She found Richard in the lobby.

"Dr. Lane, can we talk in my office?"

"Sure."

"Were you sick this morning?"

"No."

"Well, that clears up that excuse! As a partner I expect you to accept your share of responsibility around here. Mechelle schedules appointments for two doctors. I was swamped this morning. If you know that you have another obligation or appointment, let Mechelle change the appointments here. I can't handle the load by myself on short notice!"

"I understand. There is a good reason for my being late."

"I'm listening."

Richard went to the door and called Mechelle.

"Mechelle and I wanted to give you something."

Mechelle entered the office carrying a painting of a marine standing on the old ferry landing, wearing his dress

blues uniform. The soldier had been painted from a back view as he stared into the water. The inscription read:
PFC David Wayne Champion
Best Friend And Brother Of: Dr. Sylvia Champion

Sylvia hated herself at that moment. She began to cry uncontrollably.

"We hope you like it. We didn't want it to be sad, but knew how much you and your brother loved the old landing."

"I'm so ashamed of myself for jumping on you, Richard. My nerves have been so bad lately."

"It's okay. We know how hard it's been for you."

"This is the most beautiful memorial to anyone I've ever seen. I don't know what to say. Thank you both so much."

Sylvia declared the office closed for the remainder of the day. Mechelle cancelled and rescheduled appointments. Richard and Mechelle had been discussing a trip to Athens, and Sylvia thought it would give them a chance to go.

"Why don't you come with us?" asked Mechelle

"No. You two hardly have any time together away from work. I don't want to interfere."

"All you ever have is time alone away from the office! We won't take no for an answer. Besides, you need to help me find bridesmaid dresses."

Sylvia was persuaded to go, and it turned out to be a wonderful afternoon. She did find a dress for herself, and one for Stephanie. The couple chose their patterns for china and flat wear, and a decision was made on bridesmaid dresses.

After shopping, Sylvia treated them to dinner and surprised them with a pair of crystal doves during dessert. They thanked her, and then turned the conversation to Sylvia's love life.

"We need to fix you up!" said Mechelle

"No thanks. I'm quite content with my life as it is."

"We know a great guy. He's around your age and he's interested in asking you out." said Richard

"Why would a stranger be interested, unless you guys have been telling pitiful tales of my life?"

"No. He comes in the office sometimes."

"With a pet?"

"No. He's a pharmaceutical salesman. You know, Craig."

"The one with the nice voice? I think he's married, guys."

"Not now. He's been divorced for nearly a year." Mechelle said

"I really have too many irons in the fire. I'm just not interested right now."

"Well, tell him yourself. He's planning to ask you out next time he comes in."

After returning home, Sylvia called Stephanie to describe the dress she'd be wearing.

"I can't wait to see it! You did get our dresses in the same colors, didn't you?"

"I sure did. We'll look marvelous darling!"

Stephanie turned to tell her parents about the dress. Her father took the phone.

"I could've bought Stephanie's dress. We do have money, Sis."

"What's your problem? I wanted to buy something similar to what I'm wearing. I have no children of my own. Let me spend what I want to on yours. I'm buying a tent for Jonathan too, so let me hear it now!"

"I'm sorry. It's nice of you to think of them, I just want you to put some money away. Have you thought about your future?"

"Tell you what, next summer when you bring Stephanie, I'll turn over my financial records and you can see what you have to offer. I have to go now. Take care."

"Okay. I think you'll be surprised with what I can work up for you. You'll see how much you can earn over time."

Chapter Eighteen

The zoo committee held their meeting and elected Sylvia, Chief Veterinary Consultant. She couldn't have known then, how much of her future would be tied to that title.
Construction of the facility was ahead of schedule. Some of the animals would be arriving in three months. She was expected to be on hand for exams and documentation. She found that her responsibilities included approval and inspection of any animal enclosures built, and hiring a staff of animal care providers. Calling on her college friend again would be necessary. He agreed to meet with her and go over any areas of wild animals she wasn't familiar with. He would also help locate assistants.
Within two months, Sylvia had a staff of qualified personnel. She agreed only to make monthly visits, unless emergencies arose. She wasn't interested in giving up her practice for a full time position.
It seemed to Sylvia that time was racing by. Mechelle graduated from college, but still hadn't found a position with a firm. She agreed to stay on with the clinic temporarily. Sylvia offered to turn the accounting duties over to her and convinced her dad to hire Mechelle for his quarterly tax preparation. With those accounts and her regular job, she might be able to stay another year.
The wedding date was approaching, and Stephanie was coming for summer. "So much to do." Sylvia told Old Squire.
"I worry you needs a rest, Chille. Cain't jest work an' work."

"I know, but I can't seem to catch up. Maybe after the wedding, things will slow down. Stephanie is coming to stay for a while. You remember the little girl from last summer?"

"I sho' do. Nice girl. You want I be quiet agin'?"

"I'm afraid you'd frighten her, Squire. But I'll talk to you at night when she goes to sleep."

"Dat be fine wid Ole Squire."

The next weekend, Stephanie rode back with Sylvia from Athens. The wedding was a big topic for her.

"I want to see my dress the first thing!"

"Let me get into the house. Hold your horses, Steph."

The dress was a perfect fit, and she thought the pastel peach color complimented her green eyes.

"What about my shoes? Aunt Sylvia, I don't have any shoes!"

"I completely forgot! We'll find some in a day or two. Some nice white flats would go well."

"I want to wear heels! I'm old enough now. No body lets me have anything but little girl stuff!"

"Hold on, Steph! I didn't think you could walk in heels. It'll be a long day, and you need to be comfortable. We can try some and if you manage okay, I'll buy you a pair."

"I knew you'd buy them for me."

"Don't take advantage of me! You can't have everything you want here, you know. I can be tough when I need to."

"I know. I was just kidding. Gosh!"

"It's getting late. Let's eat something that's easy to fix, and go to bed."

"It's just nine o'clock!"

"I have to work tomorrow! It'll be ten o'clock by the time we get into bed."

The next morning, Richard came into the office looking like someone shot his favorite dog. He wouldn't speak to anyone. Mechelle was worried.

"Are you getting cold feet?"

"No, I'm just upset right now. I don't want to discuss it okay?"

Sylvia and Stephanie stayed clear of Richard. It was supposed to be a happy time for him, but his mood was terrible and they weren't sure what to do. Finally, Sylvia could take no more. She confronted him and found that the perfect honeymoon had fallen through.

"They didn't hold my reservations for the suite in the Pocono Mountains. I have three days till the wedding, and no honeymoon!"

"Just calm down, Richard. There has to be something we can do."

"How can I tell Mechelle? She was so excited that I arranged everything myself."

"Don't say anything right now. Let me make some calls and see what I can do. I can't promise anything, but I'll try. You need to cheer up! Mechelle thinks you're backing out on the wedding."

Sylvia made several calls to travel agencies. She couldn't get the Pocono's, but managed to arrange a seven-day cruise to the Bahamas. She asked that the agency send someone by with the gift-wrapped tickets. Delivery was made by ten o'clock, and she surprised them with the trip.

"Richard, you'd better cancel the Pocono's. Maybe we can go there for our first anniversary." Mechelle said

"Yeah, I'll do that right now. We can't pass up a free cruise can we?"

Sylvia winked at Richard and laughed.

That afternoon, Sylvia took Stephanie to the old ferry landing. They threw flowers into the water and talked to David.

"It's really pretty here. Did my daddy come here too?"

"Sure, we all did. I'm surprised he never brought ya'll. We had some good times, right here. We fished, camped out, and fought a lot!"

"Daddy doesn't talk about stuff he did."

"It's a guy thing. Men think it's not cool to talk about things we girls talk about."

"Guys are weird aren't they?"

"Really!"

Patients were scheduled thin through the wedding and honeymoon, so Sylvia could spend more time with Stephanie. The girls worked on rice bags for the reception, shopped for shoes, and wrote silly songs to sing on the porch each evening.

The wedding day finally arrived. Sylvia dressed in her peach and white chiffon dress, and wore a large brimmed hat to match. Stephanie was precious in her peach satin dress with large bow in the back. The clerk had saved the day with pump heels. Hardly heels at all, they were enough to satisfy Stephanie. Everything was beautiful, the outdoor wedding, the bride draped in layers of white organza, and the reception with the biggest cake Stephanie had ever seen! She swore never to forget that day.

That evening, Sylvia slipped out to the porch and told Squire about the day.

"Lawd, ain't dat sompin'! I never seen no weddin' like dat."

"Where did you and Molly get married?"

"Me an' Molly did'n' have nuttin' like dat. Watton able a get married like white fokes. We say our words an' jump a broom all covered wid flowers Molly pick. Some our friens' deah wid us."

"I've never heard of jumping a broom at a wedding."

"Only way we had a say we's married. No Negroes loud a get really married wid papers. We still married doe. Jumpin' dat broom wus our way."

He was enjoying Stephanie's visit. He liked to hear her laugh, and had listened to the songs they sung on the porch.

"Ole Squire wish dat girl stay here all de time."

"Me too, but her parents wouldn't allow that. They love her too."

Sylvia had an idea. The next day, she sent Stephanie to visit her grandparents, and went to Athens. After a stop by the zoo, she asked permission to take Jonathan for the night. She loaded his tent, and they left.

"Where are we going Aunt Sylvia?"

"It's a surprise."

She stopped for camping supplies and junk food, picked up Stephanie, and surprised them with a camp out at the ferry landing. They sang, roasted marshmallows, and listened to stories of their dad's childhood years. The next morning, Matt and Deborah were parked under the old willow tree.

"Hey, you wanted to recreate the real scene didn't you?" Matt asked

"I didn't know you remembered." Sylvia answered

Jonathan had plans with friends, and wanted to go home with his parents. Stephanie helped clean the grounds, and went back to Sylvia's. They'd been home only a few minutes when an emergency call came in from the Humane Society.

"Stephanie, grab my bag and your shoes. We've got an injured horse to see."

"What happened to it?"

"I'm not sure. The police are involved, so it may be abuse. You stay in the car when we get there. I shouldn't take you with me, but there's no time to take you to Mom."

"I'll stay in the car. It's okay."

Sylvia met with the officer, and Rusty from the Humane Society. They had warrants to remove the horse in question.

"What's the problem?" Sylvia asked

"It appears the poor animal has been overworked and beaten. You can't examine her till we get her off the property. Just stand by." Rusty answered

The owner, who was screaming obscenities from the porch of his home, was taken into custody. A trailer was pulled onto the property, and the poor horse was loaded. Sylvia followed to a holding stable used by the Humane Society. Found to be suffering from extreme malnutrition and whip wounds, the horse hopefully could be saved with good care.

"I'll be back with medication and some high protein feed. She needs rest and quiet. She's skittish, but gentle. Do you have someone who can take care of her?" Sylvia asked

"No, we've just got a volunteer staff. They handle the small animals, but no horses. We hoped that you or Dr. Lane could get her back on her feet. Hopefully, we can find a good home for her. She don't need to be worked anymore, but might make a good pet." said Rusty

"Dr. Lane is away on his honeymoon. I'll try, but it'll be tough coming way out here every day with my schedule."

Sylvia did all she could for the animal that afternoon, and prepared to leave. Stephanie was upset over the horse being left alone.

"I'm staying with her. You can bring me something to eat in the morning. I'll be fine. She needs somebody to be here with her!"

"That's out of the question. It's too far from town, and you're too young to stay alone."

There was no dinner that evening. Stephanie wouldn't eat. She stayed in her room until she fell asleep. Sylvia understood her feelings, but couldn't give in to her request. She went to the porch to talk with Old Squire. After hearing what they'd found and how Stephanie had reacted, he offered a solution.

"Brang dat haws here. We's got a barn. Ain't reel nice, but it be fine fo' dat haws. We fix dat other haws, did'n' we? Dat chille a hep wid em. Give her sompin impodant a do."

"I hadn't even thought of that. I could adopt the horse and keep her here for Stephanie. She'll be here every summer. You can be part owner till you go wherever you're going. You're pretty smart, Old Squire."

"I be prouda dat haws! She be fix up reel soon."

Sylvia went to bed. She felt better knowing she could talk to Stephanie the next morning about the solution.

Chapter Nineteen

Sylvia was awakened by noises coming from the kitchen. She slipped into her robe and walked slowly thorough the hallway. She spotted Stephanie, cooking breakfast.

"Good morning!"

Stephanie put the spatula down and ran to hug her aunt.

"I'm sorry," she said "I know you couldn't let me stay out there. I was just worried about the horse. I thought I'd surprise you with breakfast, to make up."

"Well, don't let me stop you. I'll just sit here and wait to be served."

"Want some coffee? It's probably too strong."

Sylvia poured a cup of coffee and bragged that it was perfect. She thought of how to handle the horse situation and decided that surprising Stephanie would be best. They ate their pancakes and bacon, washed the dishes, and headed to the stable.

Stephanie jumped from the car before it completely stopped. She was hoping the horse had lived through the night.

"Stephanie, the horse wasn't in danger of dying!"

Upon inspection, the horse looked much stronger. She'd eaten all of her food, and drank plenty of water.

"Steph, I need to talk to you about something."

"What?"

"How would you like to own this horse?"

"You're kidding, right? How? I mean Mom and Dad wouldn't let me."

"She can go home with us. I have an old barn on the property. If you help repair it, she can live there. You can come whenever you want and spend time with her."

"I love you Aunt Sylvia!" she yelled, "I'll fix the barn and take care of her too. I'll wash her, and feed her, and give her all of the medicine till she's well."

The horse was delivered that evening. Stephanie kept her word. For the rest of the summer she worked on the old barn and took great care of the horse. It wasn't long before the horse was back to normal. Old Squire was spending more time in the barn than in the house. He watched the girl care for the horse and was proud of her. One morning Stephanie mentioned that she'd thought of a name for the horse.

"What name? Lilly, or Precious?" Sylvia guessed

"No. Molly! Don't you think she looks like a Molly?"

Shocked at the name chosen, Sylvia wondered if Squire would be offended.

"It's as good a name as any. She does kind of look like a Molly. Her hair is gray and she has big dark eyes. Yeah, Molly will be fine."

Old Squire wasn't surprised by the name. He said the horse had a gentle side, like his Molly.

"Why you thanks dat chille name dat haws Molly? Ole Squire kep thankin' it in de barn till she knowed it."

Sylvia wasn't convinced that he'd had anything to do with the name, but was happy that he believed he did.

Molly was a good horse. Eventually, Stephanie was able to ride her without her being afraid. She trusted Stephanie completely and soon knew that no one would ever abuse her again. When summer ended, Stephanie had to return home.

"I promise to watch out for Molly, but I won't take your place." Sylvia said

"I wish I could just live here with you and Molly."

Stephanie slept her last night in the barn with the horse.

Chapter Twenty

Sylvia's life had become patterned. She liked the stability of knowing her schedule each day, with the exception of an occasional emergency call. Her mother worried that she would live her life alone, and brought the subject up whenever possible. At those times, it did concern her for a day or two. Richard and Mechelle gave up the match making game, and came to accept that she liked her life as it was.

It'd been eight years since she moved into the old house. She'd long since given up hope of Old Squire leaving. She thought of David no less than the year he died, and would still take flowers to the ferry landing. She and Squire talked frequently about David and Molly. Together, they kept both of them alive in their hearts.

Marty would soon be graduating. He called often to insure his position with the clinic. Sylvia enjoyed hearing all the new changes taking place on campus. Sometimes, she felt old listening to his stories, and realized that if not for his calls and Stephanie's visits, she'd know nothing about fashion or music.

Stephanie was graduating from high school. Eighteen years old sounded so final. She was planning to teach fourth grade after college. She'd worked two years at the zoo and would remain part time through college. Jonathan would start working that summer in a concession position. Sylvia purchased a new compact car for Stephanie's graduation gift. She talked Matt into the idea by bragging that if not for his genius with investments, she wouldn't have had so much extra money. She'd buy Jonathan a car when he graduated too, but until that time he would inherit Stephanie's used car.

While browsing through the card and bookstore, seeking the perfect inspirational card for Stephanie, Sylvia found an interesting booklet. Published near-by, it was an historical account of founding fathers and historical sites in Georgia. Once home, she took the booklet out to the porch to read. Checking the index page, she found "C". There were several Champion's, but she didn't recognize any of the names listed. She moved to the "K" section and found the name Kinsey. On page fourteen there was a partial genealogy beginning with J. Kinsey. She followed the chart through nineteen thirty. The chart ended. She had thought, from time to time, of the rumors that her mother was related to the Kinsey's. She'd not been eager to find proof since hearing Squire's stories. She called her mother.

"Mom, those stories of you being related to the Kinsey family, do you remember any names being mentioned?"

"No, Honey. I think my grandmother made up those stories to make me feel important. I was living in a strange place, and sad most of the time. She told me that my father's family had a connection to the Kinsey's. It was more of a fairytale, with rich ancestors, hero's, and the town being named for them. She added that I owned part of this town since I was kin to them."

"Did she know any of them?"

"I don't think so. My mother wasn't raised near my father, so I doubt it. I've never seen any of my father's family that I remember. I know they never came to see me."

"Well, we do own some of the Kinsey land you know. I traced my property through old records and found that it's part of the old plantation."

"My goodness! I guess my grandmother was having a premonition about the future instead of the past. I was just about to call you. Grandma Champion is in the hospital. She's having trouble with her heart again."

"Oh God, Mom! I'll go by and see her today. Do you and Daddy want to ride with me to the graduation?"

"I'll ask your Dad, but I'm sure we will."

Sylvia went to the hospital and found her grandmother seriously ill. She sat with her, reading from one of the inspirational books she'd purchased.

"You've gotta get better, Grandma. Stephanie graduates in two days."

"Honey, I won't make it. You come by and tell me all about it. Look in my purse and get ten dollars out. Give it to her for me, okay?"

"I will. Do you want me to pick up a card for you?"

"If you don't mind."

"I'll go, and let you rest. I'll be back tomorrow. I love you."

"I love you too, Sylvia."

Sylvia met her dad in the hallway as she was leaving. He called her aside.

"Mama's not going to pull through this. The doctor says it's just a matter of time."

Sylvia tried to control her emotions and comfort her dad. His father had died when he was young, and he'd always looked out for his mother.

"Daddy, are you going to be okay?"

"I'll be fine. She's lived a good life and I am blessed that she's my mother."

"Have you told Matt?"

"No. The graduation is coming up, and I don't want them to have this on their minds."

"But Daddy, she might not live past the graduation. Matt will be so upset with all of us!"

"I don't know what else to do. I've thought about it, and talked with your grandmother. She doesn't want to spoil the celebration for Stephanie. We'll just have to hope that Matt can come after graduation and see her."

"Are you going in to see her?"

"Yeah. I'll probably stay the rest of the afternoon. I'll see you later."

"I'm going, but you call if you need me."

The guilt was terrible. She'd been so busy and hadn't made time to visit. Grandma Champion always seemed to understand and was proud of her, but it didn't help her feelings now. She made two trips the next day to visit.

"Grandma, I brought a card for you to sign. I hope it's okay."

"You read it to me. I don't have my glasses."

Sylvia read the card and placed the ten dollars inside. Grandma Champion signed her name and thanked her.

"I want you to know how sorry I am for all the times I didn't come to see you."

"You're so busy, Honey. Matt is too. I always have you kids in my heart. I know ya'll love Grandma. You have to work…you ain't gone get married!"

"Looks like you're right!"

Stephanie graduated at seven o'clock p.m., June fifth, nineteen seventy-two. Grandma Champion died at seven thirty-five, the same evening. Sylvia had given the card to Stephanie that evening at nine o'clock. She hadn't known then, that her grandmother was dead. When Stephanie learned of her death, she framed the card, ten dollars inside, and hung it on her wall. Sylvia thought of the letter she'd received from David. Stephanie's card had come to her in the same way.

Chapter Twenty-One

Richard and Mechelle were expecting their first child. It was a happy time for them. They purchased all of the books on birth and parenting they could find. Much of their spare time was spent reading. Other than a few episodes of morning nausea early in the pregnancy, Mechelle had experienced no problems.

Old Squire offered some really strange wives tales concerning having babies.

"You know dat girl can mark dat baby. She need be careful everythang she look at an hear."

"What does that mean, Squire?"

"She look at scary thangs or ugly fokes, dat baby be marked! Don't need a hear bad tales neither. An' if she eat sompin' bitter, dat baby be bitter an' mean!"

Sylvia tried not to laugh. She could see that he believed what he was saying. Although it sounded like old wives tales, she told him she would warn Mechelle. Over the years he had told some fascinating stories. Just when she thought she'd heard them all, he would come up with something new.

Sylvia had just gone to sleep when the telephone rang. It was Richard.

"Slow down. I can't understand what you're saying. Is the baby coming?"

"Yeah, that's it. The baby. We're at the hospital. Can you come up here?"

"I'll be right there!"

When She arrived, she found Richard pacing the floor. Everything was fine, just easing along slowly.

"I thought she'd have the baby before we got here. I was so scared!"

"It doesn't happen that quickly. You've seen animals give birth. Women aren't much different, just slower."

The doctor came in and said to expect another five to six hours.

"She's doing fine. We broke her water so it should progress a little better now."

"I'll get us some coffee. Why don't you go in to see her while you can? Once they move her to delivery, they won't let you in." Sylvia said

It was a long night for everyone. The new little girl arrived at six fifteen the next morning. She was gorgeous. Not red at all; but peach colored, with a head full of dark hair curled on top. Richard was proud. He left the hospital to rest, and returned with one dozen red roses for Mechelle, and one pink rose for little Ashley. Sylvia watched the whole scene with such appreciation for life. She thought of something Squire had told. "An old soul leaves the world to make room for a new one." Her grandmother left, Ashley had arrived. It was the complete circle of things.

The clinic was extremely busy. Sylvia and Marty shared duties until Richard could come back. It seemed every animal in town needed something that week. The Thompson twins came in with their identical cats. It was almost comical to see the kids, dressed alike, carrying cats with identical fur. Sylvia was amazed at how fast the twins had grown.

"What seems to be the problem with the kittens?"

"Tara's cat needs a shot! Mine don't like shots, so don't give him one." Alex said

"Well, I can't just give one of them a shot. That wouldn't be fair. I promise not to hurt them, okay?"

"I guess so."

Tara was smiling, as she stroked her kitten. "See, brother? My kitty's not scared!"

Marty made two emergency calls and missed Mrs. Wood's dog with dysentery. By the end of the day, both doctors were ready to stay gone until Richard could return to work. Sylvia stopped by her favorite antique shop looking for an old telephone table. She found an old book of baby poems. She purchased the book and had one of the verses printed and framed for Richard and Mechelle. The verse read: "Let nothing which is disgraceful, to be spoken or seen, approach this place where a child is."

Ashley came home, and Richard returned to work. Mechelle was doing well. Visits to the office always ended in a tugging match over the baby.

"I want to hold her first! You always get her as soon as she comes through the door." Marty said

"You can have her for five minutes, then turn her over!"

Marty surprised Mechelle with a tiny rocking chair, explaining that the baby would grow into it.

Chapter Twenty-Two

Stephanie's car was parked in the drive when Sylvia pulled in. She opened the door and called. No answer. Looking out the back door, she saw that Stephanie was riding Molly. After a few minutes, Stephanie brought Molly to her stall.
"What are you doing here?"
"I missed this place, and Molly. I won't have much time with college and work, so I wanted to come before I start classes. You don't mind do you?"
"Of course not! I know Molly misses you. I don't have time to spend with her. She probably gets lonely."
"Let's get pizza and stay up late like we used to."
"The pizza sounds good. I don't know about staying up. I've got work tomorrow, and I'm not as young as I used to be!"

Stephanie talked about college all evening. She was nervous about the university, but had learned that the campus had rental stables and wanted to take Molly.

"I could see her all the time and ride her more often. I can't go four years without seeing her."

Sylvia knew that the horse belonged to Stephanie, but she also belonged to Old Squire. She kept him from worrying so much about his wife. She wondered how he'd handle losing the horse now.

That night, Sylvia went out to talk with Squire.

"Stephanie wants to take Molly. They have really nice stables at the university, and Molly would have Stephanie every day. What do you think?"

"Ain't got no say. I loves dat haws, Chille. You found Ole Squire a way a glory? Ain't said nuttin' bout it long time. I wants a go from here. I needs my Molly."

"Squire, don't be mad with me. I can't tell Stephanie about you. What would she think? She can't see you, and she'd think I'm crazy."

"Take dat ole haws! Ole Squire don't care none."

He was gone. His existence had never made sense to her, but it was real to him. She could come and go, experience new things, and live her life. He had feelings and knew that all he had was within his boundaries. He had nothing when she was away except the horse. She wondered how Stephanie would handle it if she tried to tell her. Was it fair to burden her with the secret, even if she believed it? She had time to think. Stephanie wouldn't take the horse right away.

Stephanie stayed for a week. She spent one night with her grandparents while in town, and Sylvia was able to talk to Squire.

"We're going to try something. I've never prayed as much as I should, but I'll try praying to get you on your way. I know it's been too long for you waiting to see Molly. Come over here by the swing. Look toward heaven and pray with me. Old Squire did as she said. He stretched his old callused hands as far up toward heaven as he could reach. They prayed.

"Dear God, this man has waited so many years to join you there. He's done good work for you here on earth. He lived in slavery Lord, separated from his family as a child. He learned your words even though he couldn't read, and he is kind. He tried to save the little Cotton child, and healed the sick horse. He's lost and needs your help. Please take him home with you to see his family."

"Awmighty, I's not reel smart wid words. My Molly deah wid you an' I sho' you knows her. She need Ole Squire Lawd, an' I wants a see her. I's ready now. Take me wid you."

They waited, but nothing happened. Sylvia could see the disappointment on his face. She couldn't understand why he was being left there. What more could he have to do?

"Don't you worry. We'll get you there. I don't know why you've been left behind, but my grandma always said there's a reason for everything."

"Jest don't know why de Lawd won't take me, Chille. Guess he let me know when it time. I stay here wid you while longer. I thanks ya fo' talking to de Lawd fo' me. Reel nice words you wus sayin'. Recon nobody ever did talk so nice bout Ole Squire. Lawd jest ain't listenin' dis night. Don't worry none."

Squire left, and she sat on the porch. She was angry with God. She'd made her best effort to pray and it didn't work. Suddenly she thought of her grandmother. What if she'd been left behind too? Grabbing her keys, she ran to the car and drove to Grandma Champion's house. It was quiet inside, but still smelled like her grandmother. She walked into the bedroom and picked up the boxed powder on the dresser. Opening the top, she took a deep whiff of the contents. Her grandmother always smelled of that powder, faintly sweet but not too loud. She stared into the mirror as she remembered sitting there as a child. She pulled the dresser stool out, and sat down. "So many nights I sat here while you brushed my hair. You always let me dust on a little of your powder after my bath. I loved that smell, but mostly the feeling that I was just like you, Grandma. I miss you so much."

Sylvia tucked the box of powder into her purse and walked through the house. She called to her grandmother. There was no answer. As she closed the front door she thanked God for taking her grandmother.

Chapter Twenty-Three

Sylvia hadn't taken a vacation since before college, so she planned a trip to Florida. Mechelle had suggested that she take someone along, but she wanted solitude.

On a Saturday morning, she left town. The feeling of freedom was wonderful. No telephone, no patients, just the highway. After stopping by a few souvenir shops, she checked into the Palm Haven motel. She called Mechelle and left a number then changed into her suit and went to the beach.

The ocean breeze was soothing, and she lay listening to the waves gently splashing the white sand until sundown. Each morning, she walked the beach, fed the sea gulls, and swam in the warm waters. It was wonderful therapy for a work-a-holic.

Her fourth day there, she went shopping and purchased shell covered trinkets to take back to family and staff. Upon returning to her room, she found flowers. The note read "Meet me by the pool at eight o'clock." It was signed, "Secret admirer". She called the front desk but they had no further information. She thought of people she'd met on the beach. There'd been a nice Canadian couple, an old man with a schnauzer, and a newlywed couple on their honeymoon. She hadn't spoken to anyone else. "Surely" she thought, "It's not the man with his dog!"

That afternoon she changed her mind several times about whether or not to go to the pool. She questioned why anyone would send flowers instead of approaching her in person. By seven o'clock she'd decided not to go. She would check out of the motel the next morning and move further down the beach, she thought. At seven thirty she did her hair and changed her mind again.

Sylvia rounded the corner of the building and approached the pool area. She spotted a man seated at a patio table. There was a bottle of something chilling in a bucket and two glasses on the table. She could only see the back of his head as she nervously walked toward the table. He stood up and faced her.

"Hello, Sylvia."

"Oh my God! How did you find me here? Was it just coincidence?"

It was Craig. For years she'd rejected his dinner offers when he came into the clinic.

"Don't be angry. Mechelle gave me the number. I called and found out what motel you were in and decided to take a shot at seeing you."

"I'm not angry, but this is sort of an invasion of my privacy. Don't you think?"

"I'll leave if you want. I hated to think of you here alone with the beach and sunsets all to yourself. At least have a glass of champagne before you go. People have seen me sitting here for an hour. It would be awfully embarrassing if you just walk away."

Sylvia did find him more attractive than before. She thought it might be the casual clothes. She'd never seen him in anything but a business suit. She accepted the champagne, and they talked until late that evening.

"I really need to go inside. Thank you for the champagne. It was nice."

"How about meeting me in the lobby for breakfast in the morning? Say eight o'clock?"

"Sure. I'm really tired of eating alone down here. See you tomorrow morning."

She found him to be a great conversationalist and thought it might be nice to have someone to share the sights with. For the next three days, they went on local tours and enjoyed the beach. She was glad he'd shown up, but there was no chemistry between them; no special closeness she needed to feel to have a long-term relationship. She knew he wanted more than friendship but she didn't feel the same.

At weeks end, it was over. She was checking out of the motel when Craig entered the lobby.

"Hold up. I've got to check out."

"I'll wait outside," she said

She dreaded the conversation. He'd ask if he could see her again, she'd hurt his feelings.

"So, did I mess up your vacation?"

"No, not at all. I enjoyed the company."

"I have the feeling that you don't want to continue this when I come to Kinsey again."

"We've become good friends while here and I hope that continues. I just don't want an involvement, Craig. My life is too complicated."

"You're a special person. I hope whoever comes along with exactly what you're looking for, will appreciate that. I wish I could've been the one."

He followed her to the state line, and turned off.

Mechelle was on pins and needles when Sylvia returned to the clinic.

"So what happened?"

"Sand, water, seafood, sun, oh and these souvenirs."

She pulled the staff's gifts from her bag.

"Thanks for the gift. Did you see anyone I know?"

"If you mean Craig, yes. We saw the sights and had conversation."

"I knew you'd hit it off if ya'll were ever alone!"

"Wrong! No hitting it off Mechelle. Just good friends, separate rooms, no future, end of story."

"Are you mad at me?"

"No, like I said, we had a nice time sharing the sights. In the future however, I'd appreciate you're not giving out my personal numbers."

Craig wasn't mentioned again. She only saw him on his business visits. There was polite conversation in the clinic, but nothing more. He later transferred to another district.

Chapter Twenty-Four

Sylvia had forgotten to notify Mr. Abernathy of her vacation. She found a note on her box advising her that he had her mail. She was unlocking the door, when Stephanie pulled up.

"Hey, I've come to get Molly. A friends bringing a trailer. I'm staying overnight though, if it's okay."

"Come on in. I just came back from Florida. I hadn't expected you to come so soon. Did you secure a stall?"

"Yeah, it's all ready for her."

Stephanie's friend arrived with the trailer. Sylvia walked out to meet him.

"Hi, I'm Stephanie's Aunt Sylvia. Just pull the trailer around back by the barn. Do you have somewhere to stay tonight?"

"Yes Ma'am. My uncle lives across the river. Is Stephanie here?"

"She just got in the shower, but you can wait if you like."

"That's okay. Just tell her I'll be back in the morning. I need to get on to my uncle's house for dinner."

"What's for dinner? I'm starving!" Stephanie said

"Soup and sandwich is the best I can do tonight. You missed your friend. He dropped the trailer and said he'd see you in the morning. He's very polite!"

"Yeah. We've been friends since high school. He's always been nice like that."

Stephanie offered to help with dinner, and they discussed Sylvia's vacation while making sandwiches. It seemed strange how their relationship had grown over the years. They'd become more like best friends as Stephanie grew older.

Sylvia called to Squire later that evening. He wouldn't answer. She was sure he'd seen the trailer and most likely knew why it was there. She hadn't spoken to him since leaving for Florida.

"Maybe you've gone!"

"I's here!"

"Well, show yourself. Aren't you glad I'm home?"

"Glad you's here! Dat girl takin' Molly?"

"Yes. We'll load her in the morning. Are you okay?"

"I's goin' to de barn."

He left. He was hurt but there was nothing she could do. Sylvia wouldn't sleep well that night.

Stephanie was up early the next morning and went out to prepare Molly. She loaded the saddle, bridles, and blankets into the trailer. When she tried to lead Molly out of the barn, the horse reared up on her hind legs. She went crazy, digging into the dirt, kicking her legs, and thrashing her head from side to side. Sylvia heard the commotion and ran to help.

"What happened?"

"I don't know! She must be frightened of the trailer, or something spooked her."

Sylvia took the lead and tried to pull Molly forward. Again, the horse reared up nearly striking Stephanie. Without thinking, Sylvia yelled out.

"Squire! Are you doing this?"

"Who are you talking to?"

Suddenly, he appeared between the horse and Stephanie. She fainted.

"She awrite? Did'n mean a scare her. Ole Squire ain't done nuttin' a dat haws. Haws don't wanta leave here, dats all!"

"Stephanie, wake up honey!"

Sylvia patted her face. Slowly, she came around and looked up.

"Oh my God! He's still here! Did you see him just appear from no where?"

"Come on, let's get into the house. We need to talk."

"You know him? How'd he do that?"

Sylvia took Stephanie into the house and sat her down. She started at the beginning, from finding the note in the hall closet. She told her everything she'd heard from Old Squire, stories of slavery, his wife and children, and his being trapped on the land for more than one hundred years. For two hours she talked. Stephanie cried through most of the conversation.

"This is so hard to believe. Who else knows? Why didn't you ever tell me?"

"No one knows. I've never told a soul until now. How could I have explained without sounding crazy? Mrs. Cotton, who owned this house before, is still known as the town lunatic because of trying to convince people that he was here. No one can see him unless they live here, and then...well, there are certain conditions! I'm not sure why you saw him. Maybe because you were in danger."

"I can't take Molly. Not now. I feel so bad for the old man. She's the first horse he's had since the plantation, isn't she? She must see him, or know he's there. I've never seen her act so bad. She really don't want to leave. She don't want to leave him!"

"I'm not sure what it was. It's your decision, Stephanie. She is your horse."

"He thinks she's his horse too. I have friends and college. He don't have anything. Oh God, I can't believe this! He's really been here since the eighteen hundreds? Do you know how much he could've helped me in history?"

"Stephanie!"

"Well, I would love to have seen old lady Biggers face if I'd had a real slave to bring into class!"

"He's not a joke!"

"I know. I feel like I'm in the middle of a fiction movie on channel four. Can you imagine what Daddy would say?"

"You can't tell him Stephanie! You can't tell anyone. Promise me! I have to be able to help him get on his way without anyone bothering us. He's not a freak to be written up in the tabloids. I've shared my home and my life with him for nine years. I can't explain how much of a friend he's become."

"I won't say anything. Besides, nobody would believe it anyway!"

"Okay."

"So this was a plantation, and he lived here back then?"

"Yes. He tended the horses and cattle for the owner. When he was freed from slavery he and his wife stayed on and worked. They lived in a slave cabin which sat where my house sits now."

"Who owned the plantation?"

"The Kinsey's. Strange part is…there are rumors that we're descended from them."

"You don't know for sure though? I'd feel awful if our family owned him and made him their slave. Can we find out?"

"I don't know how. We have no information about that side of Mom's family."

Stephanie asked if she could speak to Squire. Sylvia called to him.

"Sir, this is all really strange! I know I scared you as bad as you scared me out there. I wanted to ask you a favor."

"What, Chille?"

"Molly don't want to leave here. She acts scared of the trailer, and I think she likes being here with you. Could you keep her here and watch her for me?"

"Yes Ma'am! I's watch her long time now. She good haws. Cain't ride her doe. Cain't wash her neither. She know I wid her doe. She like Ole Squire stay in de barn wid her. You be comin' back. Dat what I tells her when you gone."

"She's our horse, Squire. You watch her, and I'll ride and groom her when I visit. Okay?"

It was settled. Sylvia was relieved that everyone was happy. She was glad that Stephanie knew. "A burden shared, is a burden lightened" her grandmother always said.

Stephanie prepared to leave that evening. She'd be living at home while attending college but wouldn't have much free time for visits.

"I promise, I'll come when I get a break. Squire is our secret, Aunt Sylvia. I'll never tell anybody. He's a nice old man, or ghost, huh?"

"As ghost men go…he's the best!" Sylvia laughed

Chapter Twenty-Five

Mr. Abernathy yelled to Sylvia as she backed out of the drive.
"Hey wait a minute! I want to tell you something."
"Something wrong?"
"Miss Ella had a stroke last week. Her church friends found her lying in the floor. She'd been there all night! Her son came from Washington and put her in the nursing home. Me and the wife went to see her last Sunday. She looks pretty good, but she can't move her left side."
"I am so sorry to hear that. I'll go by this weekend. Thanks for telling me."
So many times, Miss Ella had asked her to visit. She had gone several times the first few years, but not so much since. She never seemed to have time for the lengthy conversations Miss Ella enjoyed. Sylvia felt guilty for not checking on her. Trying to erase the image of the old woman, helplessly sprawled on the floor, she hurried off to work.
A German Shepard with kidney stones occupied the staff until late afternoon. He didn't awaken from anesthesia. Sylvia and Marty worked until finally rousing him. She rechecked the dosage administered and was relieved to find that Marty hadn't made a mistake. The dog had simply overreacted. She'd lost patients who may have been too injured to save, but losing one to overdose would have been devastating. By the end of the day, the dog was recovering normally."
On Saturday, Sylvia purchased a crystal vase with a bouquet of wild flowers for Miss Ella. As she entered the nursing home, she noticed two old men sitting near the front entrance in rockers. She tried not to notice the residents as she walked through the hallway. It was heartbreaking. A woman reached out from her wheelchair, grabbing Sylvia's arm.

"Mary?" she asked "You ain't been to see me since Christmas."

"No Ma'am, I'm not Mary."

"Have you seen her? She was gone bring my cat."

"I'll remind her when I see her, okay?"

"Thank you, Honey."

The woman slumped back to one side of her wheelchair and looked away.

Sylvia entered room one eighteen and saw that Miss Ella was propped up in bed between two pillows.

"Hello, Miss Ella! I brought you some flowers."

"Hey there. I ain't seen you in a month of Sundays. How have you been?"

"I'm just fine. Are you feeling better?"

"Not too good right now. I had a stroke, Honey. Some folks in here are worse off than me though. I didn't lose my speakin' like that woman over there. Thank you for the flowers. I just love pretty flowers. Can't take care of no flower beds no more though."

"Is there anything I can do? Do you need anything from home?"

"If it's not too much on you."

"Not at all. I'll make a list and bring the things back later."

Miss Ella called off items needed, and Sylvia promised to bring them back.

"Are any of your family still in town?"

"No, they're all too busy. My son came and got me checked in here, but he had to go home. His family needs him. He'll be back to put my place up for sale."

"You're selling your place?"

"I can't live alone no more, and I don't want to burden my children. I'll be fine here. They're pretty good to me."

Sylvia made arrangements with the home to bring a cat to visit the old lady she'd met in the hall. Over time she set up a group of volunteers to take special animals to the home. The residents enjoyed those visits and seemed to look forward to the animals coming each month.

Chapter Twenty-Six

The rain seemed to be never ending. For five days, thunderstorms accompanied steady downpours. County roads were flooding and so was Sylvia's basement. She rarely went into the basement. It was dark, and smelled of mildew. Squire alerted her to the rising water. She took a few steps down the old staircase and saw her boxed items floating in knee-deep water. She called her dad.

"I hate to bother you with my problems, but my basement is flooded. The water is halfway up the steps. I don't know who to call about it."

"You'll have to wait till the rain stops and the water goes down. I'll call someone and tell him to come out. Stay out of the basement till the water goes down!"

"I will, Dad. Thanks."

It was a week before the contractor arrived. He explained the needed repairs.

"You're gonna need a French drain system along the back wall of the basement. If we don't dig it out and put some drainage in, you'll have problems from here on."

"I guess I'll have to trust you. I know nothing about drainage or basements. How much damage do I have?"

"Oh, there ain't much. The wood didn't get that wet and those old concrete walls can take a lot before they crumble. We'll do you a good job."

"Thank you for starting right away. I'll be inside if you need anything."

The workers had been digging for about an hour when the supervisor knocked at the back door.

"We need for you to come see what we've uncovered."

The backhoe had unearthed some things, which were covered in muddy water.

"We didn't want to destroy nothing. Some of this stuff might be valuable as antiques. Everybody's crazy over old stuff these days," the operator said

Sylvia began picking the things from the mud. There were tin plates, a cup, an old horseshoe, and a tin box. She could see nothing more, and took the found items into the house.

"If you find anything else, please come and tell me."

The old horseshoe was pitted, but interesting. The plates and cup were wonderful examples of primitive dinnerware. She cleaned and wiped them dry, and found they weren't too badly damaged. She looked at the tin box. It was rusted shut. With a knife, she began prying the edges open. She wasn't expecting to find that anything had survived years in the mud. She supposed the box had been used to hold old documents, or receipts. The lid suddenly popped open, and Sylvia was sure of what she'd found.

"Squire! Come here and look!"

"Lawd, dat my Molly box. Where you get dat box? Dats her rang I bought her!"

"These things were dug up out back by the equipment."

She showed him the plates and cup.

"I made dem plates. Made um in de ole barn where I made hawshoes. Dat cup wus mine too. Don't member where I gots it doe."

Sylvia was excited to be holding a piece of Squire's past in her hands. Somehow, looking over the items made all of his stories more real to her. She looked carefully at the ring. It needed cleaning, but she could still see the detail. It was beautiful. The old filigree band looked like intricate gold lace, and a ruby stone sat right in the center. She understood why Molly had refused to wear the ring. A former slave owning such a piece of jewelry would've been unheard of. She probably feared someone taking it from her, or being accused of stealing it.

"Can I take dat rang when I goes a see Molly?"

"I don't know. I'm not sure you can take anything with you. I'll have it cleaned though, and we'll put it in a special place with these other things."

"We bes put dat rang back where Molly had it! You can clean it, den put it back in dat box."

The box also held an old comb, two coins, and a few crumbled pieces of paper. Sylvia couldn't make out what the paper had been. Maybe a letter from one of their sons, she imagined, or perhaps Molly's free paper.

"Did you make this old horseshoe?"

"Yeah Chille, dats one a mine. Did some fine work in my day."

"You were quite the craftsman, weren't you?"

"If you thanks I wus dat, den I reckon I wus."

Sylvia later had Mr. Abernathy build a miniature cedar chest. She lined it with paper and placed everything found, inside. The ring was cleaned and glistened in the light. She carefully wrapped the ring in tissue paper and placed it back into the old tin box. After putting box into the chest, she went to the hall closet. The note left by Mrs. Cotton was still lying on the top shelf. She felt the note should be included with Squire's items. Everything inside, she locked the chest and placed it in the spare room closet.

Chapter Twenty-Seven

Sylvia attended a dinner with officials from the zoo board of directors. She was presented with a plaque for outstanding accomplishments and service, and offered an extension on her original contract. She'd looked forward to the end of the contract, so she declined.

Driving home, she thought of her practice. Sometimes days had been hectic; animals out of control, and losses had never become easy. With all the bad days, however, came the good days. She'd made a commitment to save animals and teach owners how to ensure better lives for their pets. As she reflected, she felt proud of fulfilling that commitment.

She stopped by the hardware store and found her mother still in the office.

"Hi, what are you reading?"

"Hey. We bought an ad in this local history book. They dropped off a copy. It's interesting, and there's some information on the Kinsey's in here."

"Can I borrow it when you finish?"

"Take it with you. We can get another copy."

"How's Daddy?"

"His arthritis is acting up again. I sent him to the doctor."

"I wish he'd see someone different. He needs a specialist, not a country practitioner."

"He won't listen to me. Maybe you and Matt can talk some sense into him. Why aren't you at the clinic?"

"I had that dinner with the zoo officials."

"What happened?"

"I turned down their offer for an extension on the contract. It's been a learning experience, but my life is with my practice."

"I'm glad you won't be on call anymore. I worried you were stretching yourself thin."

"I've gotta go. I made a dentist appointment. Tell Daddy I love him."

"We'll get together for lunch."

"I'll call you."

After reaching home Sylvia took the book into the kitchen, made a sandwich, and sat down to eat. Surprisingly, she found several pages on the Kinsey family. She noticed a caption under one photograph of an old house. "L.C. Cotton home". The date was nineteen twenty-five. The article stated that the Cotton home and several others had been destroyed by a cyclone in nineteen twenty-nine. She realized that the photograph was of her land. She looked back at the picture and saw that the pecan trees were plentiful and standing in rows. Most must have been destroyed in the storm, she assumed. The Cotton's had evidently rebuilt in the thirties.

Sylvia found a listing of several Kinsey descendants. They were descended from one of the son's listed in the old Will. None were listed as being descended from James. She found that many had held prominent positions in the town, and most had businesses of their own. There was no mention of any slaves, only that the plantation had been established near eighteen hundred. "Through the years" the article stated, "the land was sold off by descendants." According to the paper dated eighteen sixty-seven, another cyclone destroyed many plantation homes, including the Kinsey's. She thought of the big storm Squire had mentioned. She was sure this was the same storm. He had told of the houses and barns being gone after it hit.

There was no mention of any Kinsey descendants still living in the area. Other information, not related to her search, was informative. There were pictures of old Christmas parades, the old building, which became the hardware store, and the old ferry landing. In that picture, the ferry was still operating.

The acknowledgement page thanked the University of Georgia's Archive Department. She thought of Stephanie. She'd ask her to search there between classes.

Chapter Twenty-Eight

Sylvia knew Mr. Abernathy had gossip, when she heard him at the door.

"Coming."

"Did you hear Miss Ella's place is bein' sold to a convenience store chain?"

"Surely they wouldn't put a store on that property."

"That's the word. Her son talked with a man out of Florida last week. They made him an offer."

"How'd you hear all this?"

"Miss Ella's son visits Ed down the road. He was in town and stopped by to see him. Ed told me this morning."

"Does this Ed know how to contact Miss Ella's son?"

"I guess. You can call him. He's listed, Ed Wells in the book."

"Thanks, I'll call him later."

Miss Ella's property joined Sylvia's, and the thought of a store going in upset her. She'd made money investing, and thought she might make an offer on the place. She found Mr. Well's number and called.

"Mr. Wells? I'm Dr. Champion. I bought the old Cotton place a few years back."

"I've seen you out in the yard down there, but never took time to stop and talk. Something I can do for you?"

"I want to contact Miss Ella's son about her property. Do you have his number?"

"Yeah I got it, but he ain't there. He's still here in town. He's at the motel, downtown."

"Could you give me his name?"

"Ben Jordan. He's a junior. I think he's sold that place. Said a stores going in over there."

"I heard, but I figure it won't hurt to call anyway."

She made an appointment to meet Mr. Jordan on the property the next morning. He was late, so she walked around the house, and looked across the property. There were several pecan trees, a line of old oaks in the distance, and what looked to be an overgrown pond. He was pulling in when she went back to the front of the house.

"Hello, Miss Champion?" Ben Jordan, Ella's son."

"It's nice to meet you. I think a lot of your mother. She speaks of you often."

"She really enjoys your visits, and we appreciate you taking the time. What can I help you with?"

"I want to buy this place. I live on the next property, and hate to think of a store being built here."

"Well I listed the place locally and didn't have much luck. I've had an offer from out of town, and I'm pretty committed to the deal."

"Have they paid a deposit or signed any papers?"

"No, that's why I'm here. I have an appointment tomorrow with the attorney to draw up the papers."

"Does Miss Ella know who's buying her place?"

"She left everything up to me. I'm not concerning her with the details."

Sylvia thought for a moment. She had no idea what the offer had been and wasn't sure he'd tell her.

"I'll match whatever they offered!"

"The house isn't worth saving. We found water and termite damage when we inspected for the appraisal."

"I'm not concerned with the house. I want the property. This is a peaceful area, and I'd like to see it stay that way."

Mr. Jordan promised to think it over, and call her the next morning. She realized after he left, that she never asked what the offer had been. That afternoon, he called with the news that he'd agreed to sell to her. She found the price a little high, but there were eight acres versus the five she bought with her house. She signed the papers two days later, and paid Mr. Jordan.

Miss Ella was happy to learn who purchased the place. She'd worried over who would live in her home. Sylvia didn't discuss her plans to have the house torn down. It didn't seem important for her to know. They did discuss the war. It was being called everything but a war on the news. She never understood the difference. It didn't matter what they called it, Sylvia had her opinion of the jungle. Word of an agreement being signed was on the television.

"It's finally gone end." Miss Ella said

"Not soon enough! They can't send my brother home. It just seems so senseless to me. All those lives lost, just boys most of them. And what exactly did they die for? The terrible things they saw over there will never go away. I'm glad that those coming home can see their families again, and I'm happy for those families who'll meet them at the airports. I just wish my family had seen my brother come home too."

"I know, Honey. I've had a lot of friends that lost kinfolks to war. World War II claimed a lot of them. Wars just war ain't it? No matter where or how they die, it's still just a lot of dying."

By the next summer, Miss Ella's house had been torn down. Sylvia had the property cleared of undergrowth, and bush hogged around the pond. A friend from the fish and game commission made recommendations to clear the pond of growth in the water. It wasn't long before the pond was clear, and stocked for fishing.

Mr. Wells asked if he might clear around all of Sylvia's pecan trees, and fertilize them.

"We could share in the profits. That's all the pay I'd want for my work."

"They don't produce too many pecans. I usually let the squirrels eat them."

"After I fertilize them with some pot ash, they'll make loads of pecans!"

"If you think you can make us a profit then go for it. I do have more trees now since I bought Miss Ella's land."

Sylvia's father began visiting more often when the pond was ready. He'd stop by after fishing to show off his catch. He usually had a story of how the biggest one got away. The pond was popular with Richard too. He brought little Ashley, but she usually called the fish and threw the bait into the water. She enjoyed feeding them! Sylvia admired Richard's patience with his daughter, and realized that their trips weren't really about catching fish. It was just quality time between a father and his child.

On one occasion Sylvia spotted her dad pulling in to fish. She ran inside, changed her clothes, and headed to the pond. She parked her car and quietly approached the water's edge.

"Got another pole, Daddy?"

"Always, Honey."

The smile on his face that day meant so much. They fished, and laughed until sundown. She bragged that her fish were bigger than his, and he laughingly agreed.

"Why haven't we done this before today?"

"I guess I figured you'd outgrown fishing with your old dad. I'm glad you didn't."

"Not in a million years, Daddy."

Chapter Twenty-Nine

Stephanie came to visit during summer break from college and had exciting news. She'd found old census records in the archives department and had copies dating back to eighteen thirty. James Kinsey was listed in eighteen thirty, but the names of his children weren't. They would have to piece together his family trail. After settling in and checking on Molly, she and Sylvia sat down to go over the papers. The census of eighteen sixty included several names under J. Kinsey. They found Amelia, James, and Sam. Squire had mentioned two sons by those names, and Sylvia suggested that Amy could have been short for Amelia.

"We need to do this differently, Stephanie. We'll have to start with Mom and work backwards to find a link."

"When was she born?"

"Nineteen twenty, I think."

"I'll look for the nearest census after that year. She should be listed under her father."

They found the census for nineteen thirty. Sylvia's mother was listed under James and Rebecca McRae.

"This is great! Now what?" asked Stephanie

"We have to find a census when James McRae was a child, to find his parents."

They found his age on the nineteen thirty census as being twenty-nine. Searching back to nineteen ten, he appeared with two sisters, Sarah and Elizabeth. The parents listed, were John-age twenty-nine, and Eliza-age twenty-five. Stephanie calculated their dates of birth to be eighteen eighty-one, and eighteen eighty-five.

"Try the eighteen ninety census, Aunt Sylvia. Maybe John McRae is there as a child."

He was there, listed at age nine.

"Wait, this isn't right either!"

"Why?" Stephanie asked

"We aren't tracing the McRae's. We need to know which McRae wife was born a Kinsey. That would be our connection."

"And how do you suppose we find that?"

They laughed at themselves. They were sure the puzzle would be solved within moments of going over the papers. Now they were at a dead end.

"We're great detectives!"

"What about marriage license? I wonder how far back those records go?" Sylvia said

"Lets go!"

Miss Abbott was on duty when they arrived.

"Back again? What are you searching for today?"

"Marriage records. How far back do they go?"

"Back to the early eighteen hundreds. Maybe eighteen thirty or so."

Miss Abbott climbed the ladder and pulled out several volumes of old books. Each took one and began their search. Within a few moments, Stephanie yelled out.

"Look, here's John McRae and Eliza Kinsey! They married in nineteen hundred. She was Grandma's grandmother. We're kin to them!"

"We'll, we aren't sure yet. We have to trace Eliza back to find her parents. She might have descended from the Kinsey who signed the Will, but I want to know if she directly descended from the Kinsey son who inherited Squire."

"We don't have census records here, Miss Champion. What is Squire?" asked Miss Abbott.

"It's okay. We have those records at home. We really must go. Thanks for your help."

Trying to keep the families' separate, and figuring dates and ages on everyone became confusing. They went back to the nineteen ten census. Eliza was listed as being twenty-five. She'd been born in eighteen eighty-five. They needed the eighteen ninety census. Scrambling through the stacks of papers, Sylvia found the census, but no Eliza Kinsey.

"I don't know what to do now."

"We can't be lucky enough for her to be on the nineteen hundred census, before she married that year." Stephanie said

"What?"

"She married in nineteen hundred. If the marriage was before the census was taken, she won't be listed with her parents."

Stephanie found the census in question.

"She's here under J. Kinsey! Go back to eighteen sixty, and see how old that James was."

Under J. Kinsey, were James M-age ten, and Sam-age twelve. Amelia was fourteen. James M. would have been the James that Squire spoke of as being a child. He was the father of Eliza. Eliza was James McRae's mother. James McRae was Sylvia's grandfather.

"My great grandmother was the granddaughter of the young Master Kinsey who inherited Squire! I don't know what I'll tell him."

"I know this sounds eerie, but don't you think it's really strange that you bought their property and you're living with their slave? What if it was meant to be? Maybe Squire was waiting for one of the Kinsey's to come back and completely free him!"

"Maybe, but right now I'm just ashamed. I've adjusted to Squire being around, being my friend. I've cried for him and the life he led. Now I know that my ancestors owned him…purchased him at auction! He never saw his mother or brothers again after that day."

She told Stephanie of the article she'd seen reprinted.

"A cyclone destroyed the plantation house, and killed Squire and his Molly. He was only free for a couple of years before that. Two or three years out of his whole life! It wasn't right. It still isn't. I see him now, in nineteen seventy-three, still wearing his tattered clothes. The calluses on his hands nearly deform their appearance, and his weathered face tells the story of too much work and worry. Maybe I am supposed to understand what my ancestors did, and try to make amends. I don't know. I know that I care about him, and when I tell him who I am I'm afraid he'll be angry and hurt with me. If the information frees him, will he leave here angry?"

"I don't know. Are you gonna to tell Grandma?"

"Not about Squire. I'll let her know that she's descended from the Kinsey's. She needs to know that her grandmother's stories were true. She always felt that she didn't really belong to anyone."

They cleared the table, and went to bed early. Sylvia thought of how to handle telling Squire. She never considered not telling him. That would have been the easiest solution, but telling him might free him to be with Molly. She knew it was her responsibility. She couldn't change what her ancestors had done, but she could acknowledge that it was wrong.

Stephanie rode Molly the next day. She stopped by the pond, and imagined building a house there when she finished college. She hoped to teach in Kinsey, but wasn't sure how her father would take the news. He expected her to live in Athens, but she loved her times spent with Sylvia in the quiet little town. She wanted to make it her home.

After closing the clinic later that day, Sylvia and Stephanie went visiting. Stephanie was eager to show her grandmother what they'd found. She felt sorry for her, never knowing her parents and having no siblings. She thought seeing some of the names might help.

"Mom, Dad?" Sylvia called out

"Come in, we're in the den."

"Hey Grandma, we've got something to show you."

They all sat down to go over the information. Sylvia carefully explained the trail from her mom back to the old Will. She noticed that her mother was crying.

"What's wrong? I didn't mean to upset you."

"It's just that for the first time I'm seeing some of my families names. They were my family, and I never knew.

Grandmother had told the truth. I think she may have stretched some of the stories, but I realize now how hard she tried to make me feel important.

They stayed for dinner. Sylvia's dad thumbed through the papers while they cooked.

"Did you see this old Will, Sylvia?"

"No, I'll look at it after dinner."

"They had several slaves, and the first names are listed in the Will."

"I guess most plantations had slaves back then."

"I think it's terrible, Mom. I'm ashamed of that information." Sylvia said

Her mother agreed that it was terrible, but tried to give an explanation.

"They weren't allowed to work for wages, couldn't buy property, couldn't read or write, couldn't do anything honey. They wouldn't have had a home if not for being owned by someone."

"All of that's true, but the first people brought here on slave ships had a home. They were taken from their homes against their will! Our ancestors participated in the purchase of those people's descendants. They bought free labor, Mom! There were many slaves in the Will, not just one or two. The only excuse for purchasing a person would have been to free them from another's abuse. We have no proof that our ancestors did such a thing. If everyone had refused to purchase humans, the slavery markets would've closed!"

Sylvia's mother went to read the Will. After reading, she agreed that it was worse to see it in writing, and to read the names.

"Put this away, please. We don't need for anyone else to see this."

Sylvia felt bad. She'd taken away the pride her mother felt after learning who she was. She put the papers away, and went back to the kitchen.

"Mom, I'm sorry. You finally found your family, and I spoiled your moment."

"It's not spoiled, honey. I just can't help but wonder what happened to those people. How were they treated? I wonder if they were even allowed to keep their children? If there wasn't so many names! It's a shame. I hope they weren't abused by my ancestors."

"I don't believe they lived as badly as some we've read about."

"We weren't there Sylvia, there's no one left to say."

"But I know you, Mom. You have a firm belief against corporal punishment and you've passed those traits to us. I became a vet because of your teaching us to help versus hurt. The grandparents who raised you, spanked you. I believe your kindness came from your father's side."

Sylvia couldn't tell her mother that she had one of the slaves living in her home, and had heard his accounts of how he was treated. She couldn't tell her that he did raise his children, and had a wonderful wife. She had problems with his being owned at all, but she'd had years to deal with it. Her mother would never understand.

Stephanie was quiet during the conversation. She wanted to tell her grandmother about Squire. She wanted her to be able to talk to him herself, but knew Sylvia would never allow it. After dinner they drove home.

"Steph, I know you think it would be best to tell Mom about Old Squire."

"How'd you know that?"

"Because I felt the same, but I know it wouldn't be fair to him. He's at peace most of the time now. He has the horse, and doesn't call out to his wife anymore. He still speaks of her, but it's not so sad now. I'll have to upset him when I tell him about the Will. I don't want to upset him until then."

"You're right. Grandma will be okay. It was just hard for her to see it in writing, like it was for us. When are you going to tell Old Squire?"

"I guess I'll know when the time is right."

Chapter-Thirty

It was nice outside. The summer breeze carried the fragrance of the flowerbeds to the porch. Stephanie had gone, and everything was quiet again. Sylvia sat on the porch, and called to Squire. When he appeared near the steps he seemed different. His clothing was more tattered, and his face more deeply lined, she thought. After a moment, she realized that it was her who'd changed. Somehow the information she held inside made her see him more depressingly than before. She felt responsible for his clothing, his calluses, and everything he'd gone through.

"How are you Old Squire?"

"I's jest fine, Chille. Molly be missin' dat girl. She be better by moanin' doe. I cawm her down. Dat girl done growed up on us ain't she?"

"Yes she has. We're getting pretty old, Squire."

"I's done been ole. Dats why dey calls me Ole Squire. Never members bein' called Young Squire. Why fokes don't calls us young, but dey calls us ole?"

She laughed. He never failed to see a different side to things, a simpler side. She sometimes wished she could see things through his old dark eyes for just one day.

"I don't really know why. You want me to call you Young Squire for a while?"

"Naw, I's use to my name now."

"It's a nice evening, huh?"

"Yep, sho' is. Crickets be sangin' an' frogs be cryin' fo' water."

"Do you ever go down by the pond? I had it cleared, you know?"

"Naw. Pon'? Ain't seen no pon'. I stays roun' here. Ustah be a stream a water run through de land. Dry up now."

"You can go with me sometime. It's still part of the same original land. It would be okay."

"Cain't leave here!"

She didn't understand why he had boundaries if the plantation had included many acres. She dropped the subject, as she'd learned long before not to try reasoning with him.

"You look in Molly box? Rang might be gone."

"No one would bother it, but I'll look when we go inside."

"How ole is you now?"

"Nearly thirty-six. We've been friends for ten years now!"

"Ten yeas long time bein' friens'. I sho' wish you know Molly. She be good frien'. She singed purtty songs too."

"You never told me that. Do you remember any of the songs?"

"She singed bout angels and glory to our babies in de night. Dey go right a sleep. Don't member words too good. Ole Squire don't sang much."

Sylvia pictured a woman similar to Mahalia Jackson, singing spirituals while rocking her babies. It was a pleasant thought. She'd always enjoyed the old spirituals her mother sang while cleaning the house, when she was young. She remembered one of her favorites, "His eye is on the sparrow." As she thought of the words, she realized that the line "I sing because I'm free" had never meant anything to her. Now, it would.

The sun went down slowly, casting an orange glow across the sky. She went inside to check on the ring for Squire.

"See it's still here." she said as she carefully unwrapped the tissue.

"Sho is purtty, ain't it?"

"It surely is, Old Squire."

"Where dat paper come from yo' brother? You can put it in wid Molly's thangs."

She hadn't thought of the letter in a long time. She took it from the closet and fought back tears as she looked at the still sealed envelope. His handwriting was on the front, just as he'd addressed it years before. She placed the letter in Squire's chest.

"Thank you. I'll feel better knowing it's with Molly's things."

Sylvia had tried to tell Squire about the ancestors that night, but couldn't get the words out. She reasoned that if it were the right time, she would've been able to tell him.

While taking a bath later that evening, she thought she heard the telephone. Grabbing a towel, she ran to answer.

"Hello"

"Sorry to bother you. Oh, it's me...Marty. I need somebody to talk to."

"I'm just getting out of the bathtub. Can you hang on a minute?"

"I'll just come over if you don't mind."

"That's fine. See you later."

She dressed, and made a pot of coffee. Marty knocked at the door within minutes.

"Hey, kid. What's wrong?"

"I don't know if you knew I'd been seeing someone, but I have. She was the perfect person for me."

"Was?"

"She said she's confused, and wants to back off for a while."

"I'm sorry Marty. I didn't know anything was serious. I had heard through the office grapevine that you'd met someone. How long have you been dating?"

"Three months, four days. Why would a woman tell a guy something like that when everything has been just great between them?"

"I don't know, but I can tell you that sometimes people get scared of relationships when things start getting more serious. If it was meant to work out, it will. Just leave it alone."

"You mean don't call her or try to work it out?"

"Exactly. If she really is just scared, and you back away, she'll have room to think about what she's lost."

"You sure?"

"I'm sure. Let's have a cup of coffee, and you try to cheer up. It'll work out if it's the real thing. I promise."

Marty was still talking at eleven o'clock. He described the girl's hair, her eyes, her smile and laugh. He described more than Sylvia needed to know, before he finished. As she listened to his lovesick explanation of why this Tina was his once in a lifetime, never would meet another like her woman, she realized how much he believed it. She was worried that perhaps she'd given him the wrong advice. What if he ignored her and that didn't work? The girl might take it to mean that he wasn't serious anyway, she thought.

"Marty, what I told you before. I shouldn't give advice without knowing Tina. You do whatever you feel in your heart is right. If you think you should talk to her, then call."

"Now I am confused! I don't want to pressure her if she really wanted to back away. I believe you were probably right."

She was off the hook...sort of. She did offer a retraction of her advice, and he chose to accept it anyway. "If it doesn't work I can always remind him that I told him to follow his heart, not my advice." she reasoned

"I hate to call this a night, but we do have to work tomorrow."

"I'm really sorry. I didn't know who else to talk to. You know how I am with my parents. I've always been a little uncomfortable telling my personal problems to them."

"Believe me, I've had the same problem with my father. He means well, but I've learned to keep major decisions to myself."

Somewhere near midnight, Marty went home. She was glad he turned to her, but was exhausted. She turned off the lights and went to bed.

Waking up was not an easy task the next morning. Sylvia dragged herself around the house, brushing her hair as she drank black coffee. She'd be a little late she supposed, but could move no faster.

Marty seemed bright eyed and bushy tailed when she walked into the clinic. He showed no signs of being upset or depressed over Tina.

"You okay this morning?" she asked

"I'm fine. I figure there's no sense worrying about it. Like you said last night, "It'll all work out if it's meant to!"

"All right then. How's the patient schedule this morning?"

"Mostly routine checkups, no surgery, one call of a puppy eating a pork chop."

"Was the puppy choking?"

"No, but I told the lady to bring him in because of the danger of splintering bones."

"Good deal. I'll go check with Mechelle."

Sylvia loved being back full time with no emergency calls from the zoo. Things went so smoothly at the clinic, thanks to her staff. They knew how she worked, and she knew the same of them. Mechelle hadn't left, even when offered a better position. She was still building her clientele of accounting customers, but somehow managed to balance both careers and her family. Sylvia looked at each staff member with appreciation that morning. She decided it was time to reward everyone with a vacation. She made calls, and checked rates for a cruise to the Bahamas. Just before closing the clinic, she made the announcement.

"I need to call a short meeting in the front lobby."

"You need everyone?" asked Mechelle

"Yes."

"I want you to know how much I appreciate the years we've worked together. Each of you has played an important role here, and in my personal life."

"Is something wrong, Sylvia?" Richard asked

"No, nothing like that. Just hear me out. I wanted to reward all of us for a job well done. We don't take enough time off. We need a break. I want you to clear two weeks on the calendar, within the next two months. We're closing the clinic and going on a cruise together! What do you think?"

"I don't know what to say", replied Marty "It'd be great. I definitely need a break!"

Mechelle was in tears. She'd been sure it was bad news of Sylvia leaving the clinic for some reason.

"We've wanted to take another cruise since the honeymoon. We'll share the cost though."

"This is my treat! I got a great deal by booking several people. Marty, if you work things out with Tina, you can bring her along too."

"Who will you take, Sylvia?" he asked

"I like my space. You should know that by now. I'll enjoy being with my friends."

The plans were made to leave in six weeks. Sylvia looked at her calendar, and realized that the week of departure was the same week of her parent's anniversary. She discussed taking them along with the staff, and they were supportive. She secured two more tickets and would surprise them one Sunday at dinner.

Chapter Thirty-One

Jonathan's birthday was coming up on Saturday. Sylvia found it hard to believe he was a young adult. Deborah called to invite Sylvia and her parents to the party.

"I'll bet Jonathan's real excited about spending his seventeenth birthday with the family!"

"He doesn't know. His dad traded off with him to keep him home on Saturday." Deborah answered

"What can we bring?"

"Nothing. Matt's having the food, and cake catered. You can come early and help decorate if you want. Jonathan will be gone with his dad between three and four o'clock."

"We'll be there just after three."

The next day, Sylvia went shopping for Jonathan. She found a male sales clerk who appeared to be in his early twenty's.

"Excuse me, can you suggest anything for a seventeen year old boy?"

The young man ran through the store and returned with several selections. He had fishing rods, a tackle box, two Georgia sweatshirts, a sweater, and a safari print shirt.

"Look these over. If you don't see anything you like, I'll bring some other items up."

"I didn't mean for you to go to so much trouble."

"It's no trouble Ma'am. Do you see something he might like?"

"I tell you what. I'll just take all of these things. My parents need gifts for him too, so I'll just let them select something from these things."

She was impressed with his helpful manner, and offered him a tip for his trouble.

"No thank you. I'll get commission on this sale and that's fine with me. You come back to see us."

On Saturday, Sylvia and her parents arrived for the decorating.

"We bought extra balloons, streamers, and cameras." Jim said

They worked fast to arrange the room and hang Japanese lanterns, balloons, and streamers. The caterer arrived with the cake.

"Oh goodness!" exclaimed Deborah "I'll kill Matt when he gets here!"

"What is it?" asked Sylvia

"Look at this cake!"

Matt had ordered a bikini cake without the bikini! Everyone looked into the box and laughed.

"I'll bet Jonathan will love it!" Jim stated

Stephanie ran through the door out of breath.

"Hi everybody, I made it!"

Deborah showed the cake to her.

"Mom, you ordered this? You're getting more liberal in your old age!"

"I didn't order this. Your dad did!"

"It's funny, Mom."

Jonathan arrived, and was surprised to see the whole family. Mostly he was surprised by the cake, and suggested that they not cut it.

"I wanted to take it to school on Monday."

"Forget it young man, get the knife." Deborah said

Everything went well. Old birthday stories were shared as they enjoyed the food, and watched Jonathan open gifts.

"Mom" Stephanie said "Remember Jonathan's third birthday party? Aunt Sylvia had to chase him down the street. He was wearing his birthday suit that day!"

"Very funny! I'm about tired of hearing that story every year!"

"I don't tell it every year."

After cleaning up the mess, Sylvia drove her parents home. She took the opportunity to tell them about the cruise.

Her mother was thrilled at the idea, but her dad wasn't sure the ships were safe.

"Dad, please don't be so negative. Mom wants to go, and I'm paying for it! We'll have a great time."

"I heard about one of those ships sinking a couple of years ago!"

"Well, I'm sure that was unusual."

"I'll think about it."

She recalled how he always said he'd think things over. He'd done it all of her life. Usually he'd agree, but it had to be in his own time. She pulled into the driveway and parked the car. Her dad exited the car, and walked to her window.

"Count us in. If it means that much to you, then we'll go."

"Thanks Dad. It'll be great, you'll see!"

The cruise was a major topic of conversation at the clinic. Everyone was excited about the upcoming trip. Marty hadn't mentioned Tina in a few days, and Sylvia wasn't sure what to do about an extra ticket. She was running out of time. The problem was solved during lunch one afternoon.

"Do you hear someone at the front door?" Richard asked

"I'll go see. The sign is up for lunch, it must be an emergency."

Mechelle went to the front and found that Tina was knocking.

"Hi. Is Marty here or did he go out for lunch?"

"We're all eating in today. Come on back to the break room."

Marty jumped up, spilling his soda when she came into the room.

"Go ahead, we'll clean it up." Richard offered

Mechelle could hardly wait for Tina to leave.

"I want to get the scoop from Marty."

"Stay out of it, Mechelle." Richard warned

"I care about him! He always comes to me with his problems anyway. He tells me even if I don't ask!"

"Well, we never know that for sure. You've never given him a chance have you?"

"Hush, they'll hear you."

They could tell by the smile on his face that Tina had brought good news.

"Sylvia, do you think I could get another ticket? I'll pay for Tina's."

"No, the offer still stands. I said I'd get it and I will."

Chapter Thirty-Two

The weather was to be sunny and mild for the next day's trip to the port. It had been a long six weeks for everyone. Renting a passenger van seemed the best solution. They would share the driving and travel together.

Sylvia was packed and had picked up the reserved tickets from the travel agency. She made a trip to the ferry landing before going home, to talk to David. She never visited his grave. To her he wasn't there. She believed that he might visit the landing if it were possible.

"David, I guess you know the war ended. They finally brought the boys home from over there. I'm sure you have lots of buddy's around you that didn't make it out either. I want you to know how much I love you and still miss you. Matt's kids are all grown up. They talk about you sometimes and I've told them so many stories of our childhood. I'm taking Mom and Dad on a cruise! Dad had to think about it, but he decided in less than an hour. That's a record huh? I have to go but I'll be back. I miss you so much."

That night, Sylvia went to the kitchen to make hot chocolate. It was a cool night, and the warm drink was good. She thought of Squire and remembered that she needed to talk to him.

"Squire?"

"Yep."

"I'm going on a vacation with my parents and friends tomorrow. If you don't hear me for a while, don't worry. I'll be back soon."

"Where you goin'?"

"On a big ship out on the ocean."

"Um, Um, Um."

"What's wrong with you?"

He didn't say anything for a moment. He just walked back and forth shaking his head and mumbling.

"I'll be coming back. I didn't think you'd be so upset."

"Ole Squire don't wanta go on no ship. Don't want you a go neither. I's heard my mama talk bout dem big ships. Fokes wus tied up wid irons. Could'n' stand up; could'n' sit up…most of um. Ships bad, Chille. You stays here wid me."

"Oh Squire. Those ships are gone forever. Nobody's tied up on any ship. The ship is a happy place now! There's singing, and dancing, and lots of good food. Don't you worry about me, I'll be fine."

"If you sho' you be awrite, den I be fine."

"Watch out for the house, and for Molly. I put plenty of feed out for her, and water runs into the trough through the hose."

"We be fine, jest fine till you come home."

The alarm went off at four o'clock. Sylvia loaded her things in the van, and went to pick up her parents.

"I'm so excited. I can't wait to see the ship!" Diana said

"Did you bring the tickets? How about brochures?" Jim asked

"Yes, Daddy. I have everything. I'll get the brochures out when we get to the clinic. Ya'll can look at them while we travel."

"Did you get your medicine, Jim?"

"It's in my pocket."

"Did you try the new doctor that Matt recommended, Daddy?"

"No, he didn't! He's just stubborn. He's still taking those sugar pills his doctor prescribes." said Diana

"I don't know why you have to call them sugar pills. They've helped me all these years. If not for that doctor, I'd be in the bed."

"Sorry I said anything! Please don't be fussing in front of the others." Sylvia said

"We aren't fussing Honey, but you know as well as I do that your dad's doctor hasn't done anything for him in years.

I think he's just scared to go to someone else and find out the truth."

"Well, let's try to talk about something else on this trip. Ya'll can discuss that issue till the cows come home and it won't change anything."

Everyone was loaded within minutes of arriving at the clinic, and it was decided that Richard would drive first.

"They'll never let us on the ship with all this luggage!" Marty said

"We'll get on, don't worry." said Mechelle

The drive was pleasant. Brochures were passed around as they decided which activities they'd participate in while on the cruise. They watched the signs as they neared Miami.

"Everybody watch for the turn off. Sylvia's driving and she's talking too much to see the road or the signs!" Jim said

"Daddy! I've done just fine, thank you."

Sylvia found the port, the van was parked, and luggage unloaded.

"Let's go! If we don't get on board they'll leave without us." Jim announced

"Don't mind him, he's a little nervous today." Diana whispered

The ship was fabulous. Painted white with bright accent colors of red, blue, and orange, her ramps were lowered inviting the passengers onboard. Everyone found their cabins, and took the time before launch to put away their things. All agreed to meet on deck, later.

When everyone assembled on deck, they waved to the people who came to see the ship off. Announcements were made welcoming all passengers, and activity areas were noted. The captain advised that the first port stop would be Nassau. Once underway they watched as the shoreline became further and further from the ship.

Sylvia and her parents went to the gaming tables and slot machines.

"I'd like to try my luck, just once." Diana said

The casino deck was like a mini Las Vegas. The Lights and sounds of the machines mixed with the clicking of the roulette wheels, was exciting.

"I wanted to play blackjack." Jim declared

"You go ahead. I'll stay with Mom. We'll be over there in a bit."

Diana spent twenty dollars and quit.

"That's it. I won't give away more than that." she said

"Here Mom, I'll front you another twenty"

"No. It's just such a waste, Sylvia. I wonder how much those machines take in a day?"

"I have no idea. Let's go see how Daddy's doing."

Mechelle and Richard played shuffleboard. Marty and Tina went to the pool. Everyone agreed to meet back for dinner. There was excitement in the air, and all agreed it would be a great vacation.

Seven o'clock came quickly. Over dinner, they discussed what a great day they'd had.

"I beat Richard at shuffleboard. He thought he'd pay me back for whipping him so bad on our honeymoon...not!"

"I'll take the challenge!" Marty announced

"You name the time, but be prepared to lose, my friend."

"We have Nassau tomorrow. Let's make it Wednesday morning!"

"You're on!" Mechelle laughed

The whole gang placed their bets on the upcoming match.

"Jim, how'd you do in the casino?"

"Oh I broke even after playing for quite a while."

Diana was behind him shaking her head at everyone.

"He didn't have any witnesses." Sylvia said

Tina whispered to Marty, and they excused themselves, saying they were tired. The others walked on deck enjoying the ocean breeze and salt air. Sylvia watched as Mechelle and Richard held hands, and for a moment thought it might have been nice to have someone special there with her. She reasoned, however, that not many men were romantics. Most would find the super bowl much more appealing than a night under the stars with their loved one. Richard was different, and Mechelle was lucky.

Port of Nassau was announced the next morning. Boarding time was given for departure, and the passengers filed off the ship. It was beautiful there. Shopping villages, open markets, and old buildings, were abundant. Diana bought a hideous gorilla head basket, which drew negative comments from Sylvia and Jim. Sylvia purchased three floral print sundresses with hats to match. Everyone else wanted to save their money for the next port. Tina and Marty did have a pencil sketching done of themselves, which Tina complained about to everyone.

"Look at my nose. It's not really that big!"

"No, it's exaggerated a bit." Diana commented

"I think we should go back and make him draw another one, Marty."

"I like it, Tina. Besides, it's not a portrait! It's a pencil sketching."

Over the course of the day, the picture disappeared. Sylvia assumed that Marty trashed it to avoid further argument. The day ended with a huge fireworks display as the ship left Nassau. The passengers cheered and danced on deck.

"People seem so friendly on the ship, don't they Daddy?"

"They're not thinking about work or responsibilities out here."

"I wonder what the slave ships were like?"

"What in the world brought that up? They weren't like this, I can assure you. It's that Will, isn't it? Don't bring that up to your mother. She finally stopped talking about it."

Sylvia thought of Old Squire and his ancestors while watching the water from the railing. She'd seen pictures of pirate ships, and passenger ships which sailed from England to the states in the seventeen hundreds. She didn't recall there being any pictures of slave ships in her history books. Squire had described what his mother told, of people being shackled with irons to the floor. She tried to put the idea out of her mind.

She was out to sea, one with the ocean and sky. It was peaceful. She sat wrapped in a blanket on a viewing deck chair. The others retired, but she lingered into the night to absorb the vastness before her. At one o'clock in the morning a ship guide woke her.

"Oh gosh! It was so peaceful out here, I fell asleep."

"You aren't the first to be rocked to sleep by the water."

She went to her room to finish out her nap. Taking no time to undress, she fell across the bed and went back to sleep.

Chapter Thirty-Three

The entertainment bulletin board announced a disco dance contest being held that evening in the main ballroom. Richard and Mechelle signed up, along with Marty and Tina.

"Mom, why don't you and Dad sign up?"

"For disco? I don't think so, Honey."

"It's not much different from jitterbugging, is it?"

"Don't mention it to your dad. I wouldn't want us to be embarrassed out there with all the young people."

"It was just a thought, Mom."

At ten o'clock, everyone gathered for the Marty vs. Mechelle match. It proved to be exciting. Several onlookers joined the cheering. The girls pulled for Mechelle and the guys cheered for Marty. In the end, the girls were still cheering, and the guys stood silent. She'd won again and still held the title.

The dance contest turned out to be no amateur event. After only a few minutes, Richard and Mechelle left the floor. Marty and Tina stuck it out until their pina coladas wore off!

"They're straight from New York's disco clubs for sure!" Marty said

The dancers had synchronized moves, seen only on television. Everyone laughed it off and enjoyed watching the talented couples. The winning pair, dressed in matching outfits, was from New Jersey. They collected the one hundred dollar prize.

"See? New York, New Jersey, what's the difference?" laughed Marty

After a few games of pool, they went to their rooms to rest for the next day's port stop. Mechelle made a quick stop by Marty's room. She knocked on the door.

"Who is it?"

"Mechelle. I just wanted to know if you want a rematch tomorrow?"

"Go away, Mechelle! It's not nice to brag."

"Just kidding. See you tomorrow."

For two days, Sylvia and her parents went their own way. Sightseeing was a favorite for Jim. He went through five rolls of film. Diana and Sylvia preferred the street shows and markets. There were local wares, handmade woven items, and wonderful pastries. The two days past quickly and they were exhausted the last day. When back to the ship they checked to see what the event of the evening would be. The marquee read "Surprise Guest". They changed for dinner and the show. Realizing that she hadn't seen Marty and Tina since boarding the ship, Sylvia called their cabin.

"Marty? Where have ya'll been? We found Richard and Mechelle after boarding. I was afraid you got left. Are ya'll coming to dinner and the show?"

"We're just resting and spending some quiet time together. I think we hit one too many bars today."

"Well, we'll see you later. We're all going down to dinner."

Seafood was served with wonderful salads, filled with island fruits or vegetables. Ample time was given for everyone to complete their meal, and the tables were cleared.

"I wonder who the entertainer is?" Mechelle said

"It better be good." Jim said "I wanted to skip this and rest!"

The lights were lowered, and the spotlight hit the stage. The Commodores appeared, and the crowd went wild. They put on a great show! Even Jim was impressed. Sylvia danced several times with two gentlemen vacationing with an insurance group from Dallas. The night ended with the last song at midnight. The lead singer thanked the audience for the standing ovation, and the band left the stage.

"Is everybody as tired as me?" asked Diana

"I sure am, Mom. Tomorrow, lets just sleep in."

"I didn't realize how exhausting these cruises could be!"

"We'll slow the activity schedule some. We have been pretty busy. Are you okay?"

"Sure, Honey. I just need a little rest."

The next two days were spent lounging, swimming, and playing lots of card games. Sylvia enjoyed spending time with her parents, but wished they would go off alone and be together. During a card game, she noticed something different about her dad.

"What's wrong? You look like you're hurting again."

"It's just my arthritis. I guess I've walked too much lately. It might just be the damp air."

"Sylvia, would it hurt your feelings if we go to our room?" asked her mother

"Not at all. I'll see you tomorrow. We have that special buffet and entertainment tomorrow night. Dad needs to rest up. You know what tomorrow is!"

"Don't remind him. I mean it, he better remember on his own!"

Happy to be alone, Sylvia grabbed a lounge chair and blanket. It was nice to sit in the stillness watching the stars, but she found herself missing Old Squire. His presence and conversation's had never bothered her. Maybe because he only appeared on request, and never demanded anything from her, she reasoned. Anyway, she missed him. It was too bad, she thought, that he couldn't see the cruise ship. It might have helped to erase the images he held.

"At it again? I can't just keep my eye on you. I have a job, you know."

"I think I can stay awake tonight."

"I get off in a few minutes. Would you like some company?"

"Sure. I was just thinking of a friend back home who I have great conversations with. I didn't realize how much they meant until now."

"Boyfriend?"

"No, an old man friend. He's been around forever I think."

"I'll be back in twenty minutes. Will you still be here?"

The guy returned, and sat next to her. He was somewhere near forty she imagined, not married, and working on the ship to forget a painful relationship. He wasn't particularly handsome, but seemed nice enough.

"So what brought you to this ship for employment?"

"It's a long story. Woman, broken heart, distanced myself. You know."

"Bingo!" she said to herself. "That's too bad. Beautiful sky tonight isn't it?"

"They all look the same after a while. Why are you here alone?"

"I'm not alone. My parents are here, and two other couples from my clinic."

"Clinic. Let me guess. Mental health?" he said laughingly

"No, that's where we need to go on our days off from the veterinary clinic."

"You a vet? I wouldn't have guessed it. A woman vet? I never met one of those."

"Really. Well, I hate to cut this short, but I need to get some sleep. Maybe I'll see you around."

She stood up and said goodnight. He looked as if he knew he'd said something wrong, but couldn't figure out what it could be.

"Yeah, I'll see you." he said

Sylvia found a message on her door to call Mechelle and Richard.

"Hey Richard. I just got back to my room, and found the note."

"Here's Mechelle."

"We were going to invite you to have a drink with us. Where were you?"

"I was out on the deck. Some insulting bore was keeping me company."

"As in man insulting bore? You're way too critical, you know."

"He's a typical rebounding bore, Mechelle. I'd rather be alone than with someone who has more problems than me.

Everyone has this hang up with my life. I have a full, enjoyable life just as I am!"

"I was just making an observation, but I apologize. You do have a wonderful life, and you don't need some man to screw it up."

Chapter Thirty-four

A Polynesian buffet was spread in the main dining hall. Fruits of all varieties covered one table in a beautiful display of color. A glistening ice sculpture of the cruise ship adorned the center, and reflected rays of light from the overhead chandelier. The next table was filled with salads, fruit and vegetable, and a vegetable tray with choices of dipping sauces. Tropical drinks in hollowed pineapples, were served by tanned, young, men dressed in Polynesian print shorts.

As Sylvia and her mom approached the meat entrée table, they noticed the only meat choice of the evening, a whole pig, roasted with head intact! Sylvia lost her appetite. The poor animal resembled some of her patients, with the exception of the red apple protruding from the mouth. The server was carving into the carcass as she neared the table. He sliced a large portion and extended the serving tongs filled with pork toward her plate.

"No thanks!" she said "I'll just have fruit and vegetables tonight."

Her mother held her plate for a serving of the meat.

"It's just pork, Sylvia! You eat bacon and pork chops at home."

"Not with eyes and snout attached! It's really disgusting, Mom."

Sylvia checked the line for the others. They'd been separated after entering the dining hall when her father stopped to speak to someone who looked familiar. Marty and Tina were near the end of the line, and didn't appear to be concerned about food. Most of their time on the cruise had been spent in their cabin, or locked in a public display of affection.

Mechelle and Richard were already through the line and heading for a table.

"Over here!" yelled Richard "We'll save this end of the table."

A Jamaican band played softly, during dinner. The music was soothing, not so loud that it interfered with conversation.

"Did you see a dessert table?" Jim asked

"Daddy, you have a long way to go before worrying about dessert. Did you get a sample of everything on the buffet?"

Marty was feeding strawberries dipped in chocolate to Tina, between sips of sangria. They were picking at their food, but not eating enough to be considered a meal.

"Dance with me, Jim" Diana asked

"I'm eating right now."

Sylvia saw the disappointment on her mom's face. She thought of how they'd been when she was a child. They'd gone dancing at supper clubs in Augusta and sometimes danced to the big band albums at home. She eased her chair back from the table.

"Where are you going?" Richard asked

"Little girls room. I'll be right back."

She made her way through the tables, and went behind the scenery of trees and greenery to the side of the bandstand. She called to the bandleader, had a brief conversation, and returned to the table.

After playing two requested selections, the bandleader approached the microphone.

"Could Jim Champion please come up and bring his lovely wife?"

Reluctantly, Jim stood up and took Diana's hand.

"Sylvia did this, didn't she?"

"Hush, Jim!"

"I understand that a few years ago this couple married on this date and danced till midnight at their reception. We'd be honored if you'd relive that night, here with us, and dance together again. I hope our selection is to your liking."

The band played "Harbor Lights" as Sylvia watched her parents recapture moments past. They moved together, as they had so many years before.

"I'll never know that special made to order, forever love", she told Mechelle, as tears filled her eyes.

When the music stopped, Jim took the microphone.

"I've loved you always. I know you thought I forgot, but I didn't. I wanted to give this to you later, but now seems like the right time."

He struggled to pull the small box from his pocket, and handed it to Diana. She opened the box as everyone looked on with anticipation. Sylvia saw her mother begin to cry. Diana hugged Jim, and showed her ring to the crowd. Three birthstones; one for each of her children, were surrounded by diamonds.

"Ladies and gentlemen" said Jim "May I introduce to you, my beautiful wife and the wonderful mother of my children, Diana."

The room roared with applause.

The crowd was asked to stay for a special guest who was being brought in. The waiters cleared away the dinner plates and offered fresh drinks to everyone. The lights were dimmed, and a gypsy woman appeared wearing full headdress and costume.

"I wonder what this is?" asked Richard

An assistant brought out a table and placed a crystal ball in the center. The lady was introduced as Kiena, a wise fortune-teller from afar.

"She sees the hearts and futures of all who ask!" he said

Hands went up all over the room. The assistant requested that a chosen passenger stand, ask their question, then wait as the lady peered into the ball for an answer. To a tall gentleman in the back of the room, she told of fortune to come within two years. An elderly lady seated near the bandstand, was given news of a forthcoming reconciliation with her sister.

"Ya'll don't believe this stuff, do you?" Jim asked

"It's entertaining, even if it is just bologna." replied Mechelle

"Look" said Richard "Tina's holding up her hand. I can't wait to hear this!"

Tina was asked to stand.

"Ask your question."

"What do you see in my future?"

The lady looked into Tina's face from behind the ball.

"I see the two of you married with a baby. A house covered with vines is where you will live."

"Hey, Marty you'll have to move to the jungle and build a tree house!" laughed Richard

Sylvia noticed the gypsy woman was pointing her ring filled finger toward their table. The assistant approached the table and asked that she come forward to speak with Kiena.

"No thanks. I don't have any questions for her tonight." she said

The assistant looked to the gypsy for instruction. She made a swift motion with her hand, and he returned to her side.

"That was weird." Tina said "She hasn't called anyone else up there. Why didn't you go?"

"It's nonsense, Tina."

A toast was held to Jim and Diana, a few more fortunes told, and it was late. They decided to retire to their cabins. As they walked past the gypsy woman, she rose from her chair, calling to Sylvia.

"You there!" she said sharply "Come here, I have help for you."

"Me?"

The gypsy woman nodded and returned to her chair. She peered into the crystal ball once more.

"Go on, see what she wants!" urged Tina

"You come with me."

"No! Only you." the woman shouted

"Wow, she's serious, Sylvia. I'll wait outside with the others. Be careful!" Tina laughed

134

Sylvia turned to see that everyone had gone. She wanted to leave but felt compelled to find out what the woman wanted.

"Give me your hands."

"What is...."

"Be quiet!" the woman said, cutting her short.

After what seemed to be two minutes, the woman spoke. "I see your spirit friend. He is unable to travel beyond your home. I will help you."

"How?"

"Come here in one hour, when everyone is gone. I will say the prayer of spirit release, and he will be gone. That is all. You may go."

Sylvia walked out in disbelief to where the others were waiting.

"So what happened? What did she say?" asked Tina

"Nothing. Let's go."

She went to her room and paced the floor. "How could she know? What if she can release Old Squire?" She watched the clock on the dresser slowly advance one minute at a time until it had been forty-five minutes. She decided to return to meet with the woman.

The room was dark except one small light near the bandstand. The gypsy woman was seated in the same chair and was putting something into a small pouch.

"Come forward." she instructed "Stand here, by me."

Sylvia stood very still, as the woman extended a prayer partly in English, partly in some unfamiliar language. The gypsy then handed the pouch to her, instructing her to place it under her pillow before falling to sleep that night.

"When the sun appears over the ocean, he will be gone! You may leave."

"But I don't understand. No one knows about him. How could you know?"

The gypsy gathered her things from the table in silence. She turned and walked away.

Walking back to her room Sylvia thought of the years she'd spent with Old Squire. The times when she had no one else to listen, he always had. The stories he shared, his innermost feelings for his love lost long before, and the comfort of his just being there, all ran through her mind. She wiped the tears as they reached her chin and opened the door to her cabin. For a while, she sat holding the pouch. It was much more than a pouch filled with potions. She held Squires freedom, and his reunion with Molly and his children. She laid the pouch aside, and dressed for bed. As she slipped between the sheets, she slid the pouch under her pillow. It was done.

"Good-bye my dear old friend." she whispered, as she dozed off.

"Wake up, sleepyhead." Mechelle called from the hallway.

Sylvia made her way to the door.

"What's wrong with you? You look awful this morning."

"I'm not feeling very well. I think I'll stay on ship today. Tell Mom and Dad to go ahead. I'll see them this evening. Just tell them I'm asleep, please. I don't want them to come in here."

"Are you sure you'll be okay? It might be something you ate last night. I can get the ship doctor."

"No. I'll be fine. It's probably fatigue. I just want to rest."

She closed the door, and walked to the window. The sun had risen over the ocean. It was bright, not obscured by anything. It just hung there, as if to proudly announce the fulfillment of the gypsy's prayer. She went to the bed and removed the pouch. Angry she'd not remembered how important telling Squire of her ancestry had been, she screamed out and fell onto the bed. "Why didn't I think? He's gone and he'll never know. It was my responsibility to apologize!" Her feelings at the moment were really more of loss. She wanted him back, wanted the friendship she'd counted on for so many years. The realization that her life would be so different than what she'd known, hit her. No more secrets, no more temptation to tell someone Squire's incredible stories, no more worrying that she'd never find a way to free him. It was over, but she didn't feel happy to be free of those things. She didn't know what she felt that morning.

All day, Sylvia's sadness was mixed with visions of Old Squire walking with Molly. By that evening she'd reconciled herself to his being gone. She even smiled when recalling how much he'd wanted to leave. "At least you gave him that." she said as she looked into the mirror.

Chapter Thirty-Five

It had been a wonderful two weeks, but everyone was anxious to go home. Marty and Tina announced their engagement on the trip back to Miami. He'd found a ring in the ship's jewelry shop, and paid way too much for it.

"It's really nice, Tina." Mechelle said "So when will this wedding happen?"

"We're going to have a quick courthouse ceremony when we get back, so we'll just have our parents and one closest friend with us." Tina answered

"Well, we see how important we are after all these years, Marty!"

"It's not like that. We're just anxious to start our life together, and everyone wouldn't fit in the probate office."

"Whatever!"

Every space in the rental van was packed. Marty and Sylvia shared the driving, and they arrived in Kinsey near two in the morning. Sylvia drove her parents home and accepted their invitation to stay there and sleep.

Pulling into her driveway the next morning, Sylvia found her house a welcome sight after being gone for two weeks. Once inside, the reality of living without Old Squire set in. She thought of the cedar box and how he'd wanted to take Molly's ring with him. Although logic told her it wouldn't have been possible, she pulled out the box and looked inside. The ring was still there. She put it away and tried to clear her head of sad thoughts.

A shower and coffee were top priorities. After her shower, and with coffee in hand, she went to check on the horse's feed. Molly looked good and still had feed available. She stroked her head and was suddenly overcome with grief.

"I'll bet you've wondered where he is, haven't you girl?"

She began to cry.

"Squire, I'm so sorry I didn't tell you. I should've told you the truth before you left!"

"Tole me what, Chille?"

Sylvia turned to see the wonderfully wrinkled, old black face of her friend.

"You're here! You're still here! I'd hug you if I could. I can't believe it!"

"You awrite? I's tole you I be fine till you come home. What you want a tell Ole Squire?"

This was it. She knew that she had to get it over with. Sitting down on the floor of the barn, she began.

"Squire, you know that I've tried to find out about the Kinsey's who owned this place. I wanted to find their cemetery, and records of where Molly was buried."

"I member you tryin' a take Ole Squire wid ya."

"I found an old paper with your name listed on it, while I was researching."

"My free paper? I show you dat."

"No. It was a different paper. It's called a Will. Old Master Kinsey died, and left a Will saying that you would belong to Young Master Kinsey when he died. Other slaves were listed in that Will too. They were given to his other children. Do you understand?"

"Never knowed bout no paper. I knowed we's split up. I stay on wid Young Massa Kinsey. Thought he kep' me cause he like me bes'. Some land split up too, but we seen others sometimes."

"Are you angry with the people who owned you before you were free?"

"Madness do no good, Chille. Live bout my whole life bein' own, no say in nuttin'. I's mad fo' Molly an' my babies, sho'wus. Thangs better now."

"Squire, I want you to know how I felt when I read that paper. I was angry, angry for you and Molly and the other slaves too. I'm sorry you were taken from your mama, sold on an auction block, and forced to work your whole life for no pay! I'm angry that Molly worked in the big house washing fine clothes while having none of her own. I'm sorry she cared for well-dressed children who slept in nice feather beds, and had to put her own little boys to bed on straw, covered with burlap. I'm angry that you couldn't earn a living with your skill, and sell your own crops, and have your own land with a nice home!"

She couldn't control her emotion, and began to cry.

"It all over, Chille. Long time gone now. Molly wid de Lawd, livin' fine now."

"You have to listen! You don't understand. I'm a Kinsey! I didn't know until I looked through old papers. My mother's grandmother was a Kinsey. She was James Kinsey's daughter. Her father was one of the little boys who grew up on the plantation! One of the children Molly cared for! I'm so sorry. If my ancestors caused you or the others to live in sadness and anger, I'm sorry. I can't change what happened, but I can't agree with those things either. If you don't want to be my friend now, I'll understand."

Old Squire looked right at Sylvia. After a moment, he spoke.

"I's yo frien'. Fokes is fokes. Some good, some bad. Massa wutton mean as some, I tole ya dat. Ole Squire ain't mad wid you fo' none dem thangs happen. You wutton' deah, Chille. You been good frien' a me. We still be friens'."

"Someday, I'll find a way for you to be with Molly. I swear I will!"

"Don't know if ya will. You might see Molly fo' me. Reckon you have same glory as Molly?"

"There's only one that I know of. We're all God's children, and we'll share in his promise of "glory". There'll be no slaves there, no rich, no poor, and no sick. We'll all be the same. If I see Molly before you, we'll ask God to let us come back together to escort you home."

"Now dat be sompin'! Ole Squire an' Molly an' my frien'. Chille, you stops yo' worry. Thangs gone be fine."

"You're such a good man, Old Squire."

Chapter Thirty-Six

The next ten years held many changes. Stephanie graduated from college, and found a teaching position in Kinsey. She married Gerald Harbin, a coach at the high school, and forgot her plans to build on land next to Sylvia. Her husband inherited a lovely home from his grandfather just before their wedding, and they moved there. Married two years, they seemed like the perfect pair.

Jonathan graduated from the University of Georgia, and joined his father in financial management. He made it clear he had no plans to marry before age thirty-two, which was his personal deadline for becoming a millionaire.

Marty had married Tina shortly after the cruise. That whirlwind union lasted only one year. He left the clinic for a position in South Carolina with an old friend from Auburn. He called and visited when in town to see his parents.

Mechelle and Richard added two children, Dillion and Alana, to their family. Ashley was growing more beautiful each year, and was sure to be a concert pianist in the future. Sylvia was always confident there would never be a divorce in their future.

Sylvia's parents retired. When her dad reached sixty-five, he sold the hardware store. Since that time they'd taken three cruises back to the Bahamas. His arthritis was still a problem, but he was forced to see another doctor when his doctor died. He claimed that the new doctor did him no good at all, but her mother argued that she could see a definite improvement. Her mother enjoyed her time gardening, and volunteering with the pet visitation program at the nursing home.

Miss Ella died in nineteen seventy-five. Sylvia donated money to the nursing home building fund in her honor. A plaque acknowledging her donation was placed in the new wing.

As for Sylvia, she was content to live in the same house with Old Squire. She did close the old clinic in nineteen eighty, when she built a new, modern facility away from downtown. Over forty, still unmarried, and absorbed with work, she had no regrets about her life. She began a free inoculation week during the eighties when rabies cases increased across the state, and received an accommodation for her efforts in helping to eliminate the problem. Several veterinarians across the state followed her lead.

She took on two young assistants, Kelly and Brittany, to help her and Richard. They hadn't taken on another partner since Marty left.

The old house was re-roofed after a hailstorm damaged the shingles. At that time, the exterior was renewed with a fresh coat of paint. She repeated the original color scheme. Mr. Abernathy commented often on which colors he would've chosen, before he retired. A new stable was built for Molly, and she seemed to like the new accommodations. The old pecan trees proved to be profitable through the years for Mr. Wells and Sylvia. Even though she wasn't sure he was completely honest with the amount he claimed to collect, she'd made enough to pay the property taxes each year.

Squire was never changing. His memories, clothing, and friendship were constants in her life. Through the years she'd wanted to buy him a new, three piece suit, but knew it was a silly thought. He'd been trapped with those old, tattered clothes, and that's what he'd wear until he left. Squire was spending most of his time in the new stable with Molly. Sylvia had installed heat for cold winter nights, and a fan for the summer. Molly was getting old, and deserved to live out her days in comfort. She'd lived a good life on the place since being rescued so many years before. Now, there was little more Sylvia could do for her. Squire talked of his worry that the old horse wouldn't live much longer.

Stephanie's time was taken up with work and her husband. It'd been several weeks since she'd visited Molly. Riding the horse had ceased two years before. She knew it had become too much for the old girl. Squire believed that Molly's condition was worse because she missed those rides with Stephanie.

"Dat girl done give up on Ole Molly. Treat her like a wore out ole thang. It a shame!"

"Stephanie has to teach on her job and she has a husband now. She knows Molly's health is failing, and I don't think she can face it. The horse is just old. It's no one's fault, Squire."

It was a foggy morning. Sylvia went to the stable to feed Molly. She'd found that the horse would eat mash better than dry feed, and mixed it each day before leaving for the clinic. That morning she added applesauce to coax her to eat. Sylvia opened the stall door, and found that Molly had died during the night. She examined the horse for any signs of life, but found none.

"Squire?" she called

"I's here."

"Molly's gone. She's dead, Squire. I'm sorry."

"You thank I don't know she dead? I's wid her all night, stood here an' watch her take her las' breaf. She wus good haws. I ain't got nuttin' in dis world wid her gone!"

"You've got me. Think of all the years before she came to live here. You made it then, didn't you?"

"Dat fo' I know my Molly wus gone a glory. Long as I bleeve she wus comin' home, I had dat. Callin her, watchin' fo' her. Ain't nuttin' now. You my frien', I knows dat, but dey wus different. Sompin' blong a me. Ole haws couldn't leave dis place, jest like me. Now she gone an' left Ole Squire too. You asked me if I's mad bout bein' a slave. I's mad bout everthang. Workin' here, tendin' hawses here, losing everthang I love here, an' de Lawd leavin me here! Making me see um all gone, all of um, ever day I sees it. Guess I's plenty mad, Chille!"

Squire was different than Sylvia had ever seen. Perhaps he'd been as angry when she told him his wife was dead, she couldn't remember.

"Don't leave and not speak to me, Squire. Don't you see that you're all I have? I've never married, never had children. Without you, I'd have no one either! We have each other don't we?"

He said nothing. He just stood by the dead horse staring at her as if he could will the life back into her. Sylvia said nothing more. After a few minutes, he disappeared.

Sylvia called the clinic, and left a message that she wouldn't be in. Arrangements for burying the horse had to be made. She called Mr. Wells. He agreed to bring his back hoe to dig the grave, and canvas material to wrap her in. Sylvia made the call to Stephanie.

"Gerald, is Stephanie up? I really need to talk to her."

"Aunt Sylvia, is something wrong?" Stephanie said

"Honey, Molly died during the night. I'm sorry. You know she's been going down hill for some time now. I've made arrangements for Mr. Wells to dig the grave, but he can't come till late this afternoon. I figured we'd bury her in the morning. I've gotta call Daddy and see if we can borrow another piece of equipment to move her with. He'll know someone."

"I'll be over in the morning. What about Squire? He must be so upset."

"He's pretty bad. Maybe you can talk to him in the morning. I'll let you go, I know you need to get to work."

Mr. Wells came to look over the sight chosen for burial and promised to return the next morning. Sylvia called to Squire, but got no answer and dressed for bed. Lying in the darkness, she tried to put the day's events out of her mind. Three hours later, she fell asleep.

Chapter Thirty-Seven

The sound of the backhoe startled Sylvia out of a deep sleep. She looked at the clock and saw that it was only five thirty. After a quick shower, she made coffee and called to Squire. There was no response. Walking to the grave sight, she passed the stable. "Poor Molly, still laying in there. Hopefully we'll get you out of there soon, girl." she said
"Mr. Wells, I brought you some coffee."
"I could use a break."
"You didn't have to start so early, you know."
"I have to leave when I get the hole dug. I've gotta meet a guy downtown, but I'll be back later."
Sylvia went inside to wait for Stephanie. She made the bed, started the wash, and made a pan of "whop" cinnamon rolls. Her dad dubbed them "whop" after seeing her mom whopping the cylinder on the counter edge to reveal the pre-made dough. She found the memory pleasant, and the rolls a comfort food. As the house filled with the aroma of cinnamon, she felt better.
Stephanie arrived at seven thirty. It was apparent, she'd been crying. Her eyes were swollen and her nose, red. She refused coffee and rolls.
"Are you okay, kid?"
"Yeah, where's Squire. I want to talk to him."
"Probably watching Mr. Wells. He wouldn't answer me earlier. You can try."
"I'll call him."
"Honey, he's really upset. I don't know what he might say to you. Just try to remember what's going on with him."
Stephanie looked confused by her Aunt's comments, but asked no questions.
"Squire, it's Stephanie. Please answer me."

He appeared.

"That horse wouldn't have made it as long as she did without you, Squire. I wasn't always able to be here but you did a great job keeping her company. I know you must be hurting."

"I's hurtin', Chille. Molly love you too. She wus happy ridin' wid ya. Guess I know you done growed up. Got you a man an' a place a work. You did'n have time like afo'. You been cryin' fo' Molly. I sees yo' face all puff up."

"Yeah, I guess it hit me harder than I realized last night. Will you stand with me at the burial today? We'll give her a proper send off. What do you think?"

"Dat be nice. I stand wid ya. Be proud'a stands wid Molly other frien'."

"Stephanie, I'll be back in a bit. Tell Mr. Wells to line the grave, but to leave enough material to cover Molly."

"You okay, Aunt Sylvia?"

"Yeah, I just need to run to town."

Sylvia returned with a huge, horseshoe shaped wreath. It was covered with beautiful red and white carnations. Baby's breath and red streamers were woven throughout. She called Mr. Abernathy and ordered a cross. "Something simple but attractive that can be delivered by eleven o'clock."

"I can put her name on it for you. I won't charge nothing for that", he offered

Mr. Wells knocked at the back door.

"I spread the canvas in the grave. How are you gone get her in there?"

"I have a forklift on the way. We'll have to harness her and put her on the forks."

"Hope it's a big lift!"

"Thanks for your help. I'll get you a check."

"I don't want no money. I liked that old horse. I used to go in and talk to her when I came to work the trees. Helping to put her to rest is my gift."

Harnessing the horse was difficult. It took the forklift operator, Stephanie, and Sylvia to secure the straps and roll her over. By ten thirty they had her balanced on the forks ready to move to the grave sight. Slowly, the operator moved toward the opening. He carefully tilted the forks downward, and Molly slid into the hole with a loud thud!

"Oh Molly!" cried Stephanie "I'm sorry."

As the operator pulled away, Sylvia saw Mr. Abernathy approaching. She ran to stop him near the house.

"Stephanie is really upset. I'll just take this so she can spend a few minutes alone. Can I pay you tomorrow?"

"That's fine. Hope it's what you wanted. I cain't be real detailed on short notice, you know. You need to seal that wood with something to protect it from the rain."

"I will. It's beautiful, Mr. Abernathy. Thank you so much."

"You puttin' that horse in the ground out there?"

"Yes. We've lined the grave, it'll be fine."

"I figured you'd just haul her off and burn her or something."

"I couldn't do that to Stephanie."

Sylvia took the cross into the house. He'd done a good job. The edges had been burned to give a finished look, and the name was carefully burned into the front of the cross. The lettering resembled old English style. It was missing one important thing, she thought. Opening the cedar box, she found the old horseshoe Squire had made years before. With hammer and nail, she placed the horseshoe on the top of the cross. She returned to the grave sight as Stephanie and Squire were paying tribute to their horse.

"She reel good haws fo' me ten' to. I thanks ya Lawd fo' lettin' me know her."

"If there is a horse heaven, dear Lord, then see to it that this one gets a special stable. We'll miss you, Molly."

"We need to call Mr. Wells, Steph. Help me fold the material over her, then run and call for me, okay?" Sylvia said

They carefully covered the horse as Squire looked on. Stephanie went to the house to make the call.

Sylvia picked the cross up from the ground.

"Squire, I thought she should have something from you. This is your old horseshoe. You don't mind do you?"

"No Ma'am, I sho' don't. Makes me proud'a give it to her. I thanks ya fo' puttin' it on dat cross."

Mr. Wells filled in the grave with concrete. The flowers and cross were placed on top.

"Aunt Sylvia, where'd you get that cross?"

"Mr. Abernathy made it for me this morning."

"Where did the horseshoe come from? It's pretty rusty."

"It's a long story. I didn't realize I never told you. Sometime when we can get together, I will."

The stable stood sadly empty. Sylvia later suggested getting another horse, but Squire didn't want another horse in Molly's stable.

"Don't thanks I can ten' no more hawses. I tired of um. Dey like fokes. You watch um long time, den dey leaves. I's lost too much, don't wanta lose no moe."

Several months later, Sylvia had a plaque made, and hung it in the stable. The plaque read:

"Molly"-Owned by:

Squire Kinsey and Stephanie Champion Harbin

A painting of Stephanie, riding Molly, was hung on the back wall of the stall. The stable would be a shrine to Molly, and a comfort to Old Squire.

Chapter Thirty-Eight

There was a change in Squire after the horse died. His conversations of old times became more of bad memories. Some stories of his life on the plantation, he'd never shared. Now, he was recanting those.

"One day it wus so hot in de fields. Mans, boys, women, all foke wus fallin' out. My boy, Levi, he falled out three times. Field boss jest make him kep workin'. Dat night he be so sick. Molly thought he jest die fo' moanin' Next day he had'a go right back a dem fields. My boy, Jabo, work wid em an' done both dey work when boss not lookin. Dat time, one time me an' Molly get mad. We knowed we brung slave babies in dis world an' we wus mad ourselves fo' dat. Molly stood up tall in de big house bout her boy. Tole Massa wife he be sick an' fokes be fallin out. Massa wife did'n say nuttin' sept she sorry. Miss Amy, she tole her daddy stop de work fo' three days, else she run clear way from him an' never come back! Work stop too. Three day rest fo' all field foke."

"You never told me your son's names. Where did Jabo get his name?"

"It really Jacob. I call em Jabo."

"I hope they found good jobs up north after the war and lived happy lives."

"Dey hard workers. I sho' somebody proud'a have um work wid um."

"Did they take the Kinsey name?"

"Yeah, we sign ours name affah de war. Levi put my name bein' Kinsey an' deys too. Lotta slaves taked Massa name."

Sylvia wondered if his descendants could be traced to find any living relatives. She wanted his and Molly's things to go to their family if possible.

"Do you know where they went up north?"

"Naw, Jest nawth."

She made note of the names he had mentioned.

Every conversation with Squire seemed to end with his wanting out. No longer content to stay with her, he'd pace the floor and talk angrily about being left behind. He'd yell out for God to take him and receive no answer. Sylvia knew he needed his family to ever be at rest.

Sylvia researched the library for any slave records, but found nothing useful. The state archives did have a registry of slaves dated eighteen sixty-six. Listed on that registry were Squire, Molly, Levi and Jacob. No information on where they went from that point was noted. She talked with the historian on duty.

"Some have been able to trace through northern records. You'd have to check with Boston, or New York. Some factories did keep records of blacks who worked near the turn of the century."

Disappointed, she went home. A trip up north wouldn't be possible. She'd missed time, and put extra work on Richard when Molly died. Correspondence by mail seemed the best solution. She wrote letters to state archives divisions in several northern states. She told Squire of her plan to find his grandchildren.

"I'm trying to locate some of your grandchildren. If I can trace Levi or Jacob, they may have grandchildren that could come here and visit."

"Don't make no sense. Dem boys ain't comin' back here. Said dey watton'!"

"I thought you'd be happy to see someone who's kin to you and Molly."

"Done tole ya. Levi an' Jabo all we had an' dey ain't been back here. Ain't comin' now."

She realized that he thought Levi and Jacob were still alive and working up north. She didn't try to explain.

Sylvia made calls to secure addresses, and was advised of a two to three month response time by most of the archives departments. She mailed the paperwork.

It had been only six weeks when Sylvia received her first reply from Boston Archives Department. Scanning the information, she searched for the names Levi or Jacob. On the second page, she found Jacob Kinsey. He had worked in Boston, at age sixty-two. On the "Family members" page, she found the names Isaac, Jacob, Esther, and Rubin-children of Jacob Kinsey (page 2). There was information on children, Jacob and Issac. They'd worked for an iron works plant and lived near Philadelphia. No information on other children was listed. Sylvia estimated ages of the two sons found, at somewhere between thirty and forty. If they were born after nineteen hundred, she hoped to find them listed on census records. Turning the page, she found that her work had been done for her. Isaac was listed on the nineteen ten census as a Negro man. No mention of family or age. There were no further census records found. Perhaps he moved, she thought, and was on another state's record.

Over the next few weeks other replies came in the mail. "No information on persons requested" became familiar reading. She decided to take the information on Isaac and search further. Eliminating states through rejection letters received, she wrote to the Carolinas, hoping the family moved back to the south.

After hearing nothing for several months Sylvia lost interest in the search, and thought no more of it.

Chapter Thirty-Nine

Richard met Sylvia at the door of the clinic as she approached one morning.
"Telephone for you."
"You couldn't help them?"
"No, not this one."
"Hello"
"Hey Lady, it's been a long time."
"Who's calling please?"
"An old friend, I think. I can't remember how I left it."
"I'm sorry, please be a bit more specific. I'm really busy."
The caller hung up. She thought of who it might have been, and Craig came to mind. "No" she thought, "It wasn't his voice." His had been very distinguishable.
"Two neuters, one de-claw, and a stray covered with ticks." Mechelle said as she handed over the files.
"Where'd the stray come from?"
"Animal control brought it in. They wouldn't take her with the tick infestation."
"She out back or in a kennel?"
"Kennel."
Kelly brought the poor animal into the exam room and Sylvia began the tedious task of removing the bloodsuckers one at a time.
"She's a nice dog. I hate to see her go to the shelter. She's about four or five years old, and a collie mix. It's doubtful she'll find a home at her age."
"What happens if they don't find a home for her?" Kelly asked
"They'll euthanize her in seven days."
Mechelle came to the door.
"I think you need to come up front."

"Problem?"

"Maybe, I can't say for sure. That's your call."

"Sylvia walked into the lobby and looked around the room. She saw patients with their owners, but no apparent problems. Turning to check with Mechelle, she spotted Chuck standing behind the partition. He stepped out.

"My god, it is you. Did you call earlier?"

"Yeah, I decided to drop by instead of telling you who I was. I went to the old building, and found you'd moved. This is nice. You haven't changed much over the years. Ever get married?"

"No, never found the time. How about you?"

"Yeah, I've been married for a while now. I have a son ten years old."

He pulled out the pictures of his son and wife. She politely nodded as she looked at them. His wife looked young, she thought, and probably was very naive when she met him.

"So, did you miss me when I left?"

"Not that I recall."

Suddenly, she felt all the emotion of a time past. The humiliation she'd suffered that last night with him came back.

"You want'a get together later? I'll buy your dinner."

"Don't think so! I'm not as charitable as I used to be. I'm more selective these days. Perhaps you should just grab a sandwich and call your wife. I have some ticks waiting in the exam room, if you'll excuse me. Nice to see you again."

The look on his face said it all. He was humiliated. She'd waited all those years to pay him back and finally had the chance. She felt good.

"Dr. Champion" Kelly said "Don't let them kill her. I'll take her home with me. She's a good dog."

"She probably needs shots and an exam, Honey."

"I'll pay for it. Just don't let them kill her."

After a bath and clip, the dog looked much better. She was slightly malnourished, but okay.

"What's her name?" Kelly asked

"No name, you'll have to give her one."

"I'll think it over. Maybe after I see her personality for a day or so."

Richard commented on Kelly's inability to let the dog go.

"She'll take everything that comes through the door without an owner."

He wasn't totally correct. She did take several, but was really good at finding great homes for most, through the years.

Sylvia checked her mail after forgetting for a few days. She didn't like the new mailman. She didn't even know his name. Over the years she'd complained about Mr. Abernathy's gossip problem, but now she wished he was still around. He always left reminder notes when she didn't check her mail, and was friendly. Thumbing through the stack of mail, she found an envelope from South Carolina Genealogy Society. Inside, there was information on Isaac Kinsey. He'd moved back to the south, and appeared on the nineteen twenty census. There was only one child listed named Esau. No mention of a wife. The child was eighteen. Information on Esau followed. Wife; Essie, and children: Issac, Walter, and Purcell. No age or reference on any of them. Information from public records sources, the letter said. Sylvia wrote down all names, and estimated that Esau's children would have been born between nineteen twenty and nineteen thirty.

From information received that day, Sylvia did find a trail of Squire's descendants. It led to Esau's grandson, Walter Jr. He was in Sumpter County, South Carolina under Walter Kinsey Sr.'s name. His mother was Ruby. At the time of the census, he was two years old. His father was listed as being twenty-five. They all disappeared by the nineteen eighty census. She had them up till the sixty's! She prepared letters to each of them explaining that information on their ancestors- Squire and Molly Kinsey, was available. She listed her name, address, and telephone numbers. The post office suggested that she send the letters general delivery to post offices in their area, as she had no correct addresses. She marked each with instructions to forward to last known address.

Chapter Forty

In March nineteen ninety, Sylvia lost her father. It was perhaps her deepest loss ever. For days she didn't work, didn't leave the house. She lost fifteen pounds and couldn't seem to find her appetite. Old Squire was with her during those days. He talked and paced the floor not knowing what to do. He stopped complaining or speaking of his desire to leave. His friend was in pain, and she was more important.

Sylvia's mother took the news better than expected. Matt thought she was only doing what she'd always done, being strong for everyone else. She visited each day, bringing soups and custards, in an attempt to encourage her daughter to eat.

"Baby, you have to eat something. Daddy wouldn't want you like this. Please try to eat a little."

"Mom, I know I need to eat, need to snap out of it, get on with life! I'm fifty-two years old and I've lost other family! None of that helps! You'd better not leave like Daddy and David."

"What does that mean? We'll all leave at some point, Sylvia."

"I never even had a chance to say good-bye to them. I just got a call saying they'd died, Mom. It's not fair. I had more to say to him!"

"Honey, your dad had a sudden heart attack. There was no warning, no time for phone calls or good-byes. You should be happy that he didn't suffer. I'm shocked that you've turned your sorrow into something more about yourself than your dad."

"Mom, just leave. Please!"

Sylvia was angry that her mother made her sound selfish and self-absorbed. She had loved her dad and was grieving for him.

"Chille" Squire said "I knows you hurtin' fo' yo daddy. I listen a you cryin' an' watch you not eatin' nuff a keep a field mice alive. When I heard my Molly left me an' wus awready gone a glory, I said same thang. "Why she left me?" Didn't thank about her. Yo' mama right Chille. We thanks bout us, like Molly an' yo' daddy die outah spite or sompin'. We be wrong."

Sylvia listened. For the first time since the funeral, she cried for her father, instead of herself.

"Squire you're right. We need to grieve that they're gone, but celebrate the times we spent with them. Thank you for helping me to see that."

She showered, dressed, and went to see her mother. They talked about the happiness her father had brought to the family.

"I'm sorry Mom, for the way I've acted. I was being selfish, and didn't see it."

"Sweetheart, we all handle things differently. I'm glad that you're okay now."

"I think I could eat some of that egg custard, if you still have some."

"I'm sure I can scrape up a dish full."

After that day, Sylvia spent many wonderful days with her mother. Whenever she took short trips, she took her along. She wanted no regrets of time not spent or things not said, with her.

While visiting her mom one afternoon, Stephanie and Gerald came to announce that they were to be parents. They had given up on having their own children years earlier, and put their name on a list for adoption. They'd just received word that a baby girl had been born in Texas, and they were flying out to pick her up.

"We have to hurry. We just wanted to tell you before we left."

"Stephanie, I'm so happy for both of you. And for that lucky little girl!" Sylvia said

Upon Stephanie's return, everyone gathered at the airport to see the new baby.

"We've named her Ariel!" Gerald announced

She was a pretty baby, with dark hair and expressive eyes. She brought new hope and joy into the family at a time they needed both. The loss of Sylvia's dad had been hard on the family, but Matt showed no signs of sadness that day. He was a new grandfather!

A celebration welcoming Ariel into the family was held that evening. Stephanie and Gerald had decorated a nursery three years before, in hopes of one day having a child to place there. The room was bright, with pale yellows and white. Stephanie's grandmother had crocheted a baby coverlet in colors of yellow, green, pink and blue. It lay gracefully at the foot of the baby bed. Teddy bears of different sizes and colors lined the wall shelves, and Grandma Champion's rocker sat waiting for the baby.

Sylvia tiptoed into the nursery to see Ariel one more time before leaving. She touched the tiny little hand and stood quietly, watching her sleep.

"When you get older, you're mommy will buy you a pony and name her Molly. She'll teach you to ride and to love animals the way she did."

She turned to find Jonathan standing in the doorway. He was such a man now. She thought of his plans from the past.

"I do believe that you are now over thirty-two. Where's that bank statement? I want to look at those six digits!"

"I didn't make it by thirty-two. It seemed possible back then but I didn't realize how hard it is to reach your goals."

"Son, you set a mighty high goal for yourself. You may make it by fifty, but thirty-two was a bit unlikely for anyone! Are you seeing anyone seriously?"

"Everything I do is serious, Aunt Sylvia. If you mean do I have plans to marry, no."

"Okay, I'll quit asking questions. You could come visit once in a while you know!"

"I would, but I'm too busy. Got to make that million remember?"

After dropping her mother off, Sylvia went home and sat on the old porch swing. Like an old woman, it seemed to creak more with age, she thought. She reflected on all the years she'd spent in the house, and thought of Miss Ella's touch-me-nots. She still harvested the seed each year.

"Squire"

"What you want, Chille."

"Just wanted to know you're here, I guess. I was thinking of how many years we've spent talking on this old porch. You should see Stephanie's baby. She's precious, and has these big, dark eyes that make you want to grab her and hold her."

"She gone be comin' here a see us?"

"You know her mama will bring her. We're closer than anyone to her."

"Hope dat baby be sweet like it mama."

"I'm still looking for some of your grandchildren. They were in South Carolina, but I lost track of them. I've written letters, and maybe I'll find at least one of them."

"Why you want'a do dat? Won't do Ole Squire no good. Cain't talk to um, cain't be wid um."

"You could see them if they came here. You might not be able to talk to them, but I could. You could tell them anything you wanted, through me. What about Molly? Don't you think she'd want you to see them?"

"Don't know dat. She ain't here a tell me nuttin' bout it."

"Well, I might not hear from them anyway. We won't worry about it till I do."

They stayed on the porch listening to the frogs and crickets until late that night. She wouldn't mention the relatives again unless she found them, and knew they were coming to visit.

Chapter Forty-One

Ashley was graduating from high school. She was eighteen years old and on her way in the world. She received a full scholarship to Julliard Music School to study concert piano. Her path toward that goal had been set many years before, when her piano teacher realized her potential. Throughout her life, Sylvia had attended each spring concert, always in awe of the child's ability.

The graduation was held in the school auditorium. Sylvia met Mechelle and Richard inside, and sat with them near the front. After speeches by school officials, and special awards presentations, Ashley was asked to come up and play a selection for the audience. Mechelle cried as her daughter began to play.

"I'm so proud of her, Sylvia. She's been such a blessing to us. Just listen to her. It's pretty amazing huh?"

"It's wonderful, Mechelle! You and Richard have done a great job of supporting her music and encouraging her to be the best."

When Ashley completed the piece, she was surprised and honored with a presentation. A representative of Julliard presented her scholarship. Ashley cried and thanked the presenter, then took a moment to acknowledge her parents as her best audience and constant source of encouragement. It was a touching moment for everyone.

When the caps were thrown into the air and the students roared with cheers, it was over.

Everyone went back to the house to wait for Ashley and her friends, who'd been promised a steak dinner. Sylvia gave Ashley her gift when she arrived.

"I hope you can use these."

Ashley opened the package to find a clock radio and a pair of gold earrings.

"I'll need this clock when I go away to school, and the earrings are beautiful. Thank you!"

"You're very welcome, Ashley. I'm very proud of you. I'm going to slip out now, if you don't mind. I promised to go by Stephanie's tonight."

"Tell her I said hello."

"Sylvia!" someone called as she entered her car.

She stepped out to see Marty. He looked so much more mature.

"I saw you leaving the graduation, but couldn't catch you. It was great wasn't it? Our little Ashley all grown up and so talented."

"Does Mechelle know you're here?"

"No, I got in just as the graduation was starting."

They went into the house together. Sylvia didn't want to miss the reunion.

"Mechelle, look what I found in the yard."

Expecting to see a stray animal, Mechelle came into the room. Marty ran and picked her up off the floor.

"Did you see Ashley graduate? We didn't see you there."

"Yeah, I got there late. I caught the performance and everything though. Where are the other kids? I've never even met the youngest one."

"We're grilling out back. Ya'll come on out there. Richard will be so glad to see you.

It was great to be together again. They talked about Marty being the baby of the group, and how much they'd missed him. He'd still not married again, but was dating a woman who had three children.

"I'm not sure how it'll work out. We're just having a good time right now and enjoy each other's company."

"Well, I hope you'll be more careful this time. But a woman with three kids? The kids might not want someone with their mom permanently." Mechelle said

"Mechelle, you're doing it again, and he just got into town." Richard cautioned

"I was so sorry about your dad, Sylvia. He was great on that cruise, wasn't he?"

"Yeah, he was. We appreciated your flowers. They were nice. I always thought we'd take another cruise together, but it didn't work out."

"Tina screwed everything up!" said Mechelle

Richard cautioned her again to go easy on touchy subjects.

"Did you guys think the divorce made me decide to leave town? That wasn't it. I needed to get away from my parents. They wouldn't let me be on my own. They've eased up over the years. Tina moved right after the divorce too. She's married to some guy in the military, and has kids and everything. My mother ran into her a year or so ago."

"Are you happy where you are?" asked Sylvia

"It's okay, I guess. The customers are more middle to upper class, and not as friendly as here. I haven't been offered any squash or fresh tomatoes since I left the old clinic."

Before leaving, Sylvia invited Marty to come by her house the next day. It was good to see him doing so well. Once home, she called Stephanie to check on the baby.

"Hey Sweetie, how's my favorite mother and child?"

"We're fine. She's not sleeping too well, but Gerald's been great at swapping out feedings. I thought you'd stop by after the graduation. How'd it go?"

"It was unbelievable! Ashley was asked to perform, and a representative from Julliard presented her scholarship. I was on my way to your house when Marty showed up. I couldn't leave then."

"I want to see him while he's here! I had such a crush on him when I was thirteen. Did you tell him about the baby?"

"No, we're going to surprise him tomorrow. He's coming for lunch. Can you and Gerald bring the baby about eleven?"

"Sure. This is great! I know he thought I'd never be a mother."

"Well, I'll see you at eleven tomorrow."

Casseroles seemed best to avoid standing in the kitchen all morning. Sylvia made several casseroles, and a fruit medley. The rolls were almost brown when Stephanie knocked at the door.

"Let me get the rolls out! I'll be right there. Come in and hand over my baby. I haven't seen you in three days!"

Gerald went to the front room and turned on the television. Stephanie went to check the menu then offered to make tea.

"When did Marty say he'd be here?" Stephanie asked

"He said eleven thirty. What time is it?"

"Eleven thirty-one."

Sylvia heard the telephone ring, but had her hands full with Ariel. Stephanie answered.

"Is this Marty? Yes Sir, but I'm her niece. Hold on, and I'll get her."

Sylvia took the telephone from Stephanie and handed over the baby.

"Hello, this is Sylvia."

"My name is Walter Kinsey. I received a letter about some of my ancestors. Could you tell me what this is about?"

"I have information on your ancestors which might be interesting to you and your family. It's a little hard to explain over the phone. Where are you calling from?"

"I live in Fairview, South Carolina. It's just over the state line from Georgia. I think you have the wrong family, Ma'am. I've talked with my uncle and some cousins. No one has ever heard of a Squire or Molly Kinsey. Our family came from up north."

"Why don't we plan to meet and discuss this? It would be great if you could come here, say next weekend?"

"I'm willing to hear what you have to say, but I really don't think I'm from that family."

Sylvia gave directions and wanted to scream with excitement as she hung up the telephone. Remembering that Gerald was sitting in the room, she kept quiet.

Marty arrived fifteen minutes late. He was more than surprised to see that Stephanie had become a mother.

"I know how long you've waited for this, kid. She's beautiful."

While the men played with the baby, Stephanie went to the kitchen to talk to Sylvia.

"Who was on the telephone? Was it something to do with Squire?"

"I located a descendant; Walter Kinsey. He's coming next weekend. I thought I'd never find anyone. It's been one dead end after the other", whispered Sylvia

"What are you going to say?"

"I don't know for sure. I want to see him face to face, first. I want someone to have Molly's box; someone who's really kin to her."

"What box?"

"We need to talk when nobody can hear us. I was going to tell you when the horse died. I guess I never did. Remember the old horseshoe?"

"The one on the grave?"

"It belonged to Old Squire in the eighteen hundreds. We found some other things too. I don't want to get caught talking. I'll tell you everything later."

"You better! We've been in this together, you know."

Dinner was ready, and the guys came in to get a plate. Sylvia wouldn't have a chance to talk to Stephanie again that day. They agreed to meet for lunch the next Tuesday. Stephanie didn't think she could live until she heard the story.

Chapter Forty-Two

Sylvia stepped out into a puddle of ankle deep red water. Looking to see if anyone noticed, she hurried through the downpour to the restaurant door. After a quick stop by the rest room to clean her shoes, she joined Stephanie in a booth near the back of the room.

"I forgot about the parking lot when I suggested this place! It's fine unless it rains, then the red clay comes up through the gravel!"

"I parked on the grass around back."

"How's the baby this morning?"

"She's great. She slept better last night. Grandma was excited when I asked her to baby sit for a while."

"I know she misses having someone to take care of. She'll enjoy the baby."

The waitress took their dinner order, and brought iced tea.

"Now tell me, what's all this mystery about Squire?"

"You remember the basement leaking and I hired someone to dig a drain against the back wall?"

"I think so."

"Well, they dug up some old things including a tin box. The box contained the old ring that Squire gave Molly, and some other trivial items."

"I don't remember about any ring."

"Amy Kinsey ordered it for Squire out of a catalog, after he'd seen it. She never wore it, just kept it in that tin box."

"Oh my God! You have that ring? Why didn't you tell me?"

"I don't know. I'm not sure what I've told you through the years. Anyway, I wanted to find someone to leave that ring to, if anything happens to me."

"So you're giving the ring to that man?"

"No, Squire would be furious! He thinks he'll be able to take it to Molly. I'm sure he couldn't, but I can't tell him that. He asks to see the ring from time to time. It has to stay in the house until I leave, but after that I wouldn't want anyone else to find it."

"Can you imagine how we'd feel if somebody found something that old from our ancestors?"

"That's why I feel so strongly about this. Most descendants of slaves have nothing. There's no record of where most of them went after the war."

"Are you going to tell the man that you're kin to the Kinsey's?"

"I sure am!"

"What if he gets angry, Aunt Sylvia? Is he bringing other family with him?"

"I don't know. I believe that not owning who we are, and that our ancestors participated in slavery, would make him more angry."

"You can't change history, you know. I feel the same way you do, but what good would it do now?"

"Maybe I can't change history, but my apology or at least my disagreement with that part of history, might ease the anger and hurt of one or two of Squire's grandchildren."

"I hope you're right and things turn out like you want. Maybe I need to be there with you, just in case."

"I really think I need to handle this alone. I'll have Squire with me."

"If you aren't going to give him the box, what proof are you going to give him? He can't see Squire."

"I have the Will, and record of where Squire's sons and grandsons lived. The family line is documented down to this guy."

"Will you call me if you need me? Call me anyway and let me know what happens."

The waitress brought the dinners.

"Sure, now eat up. We're going shopping. I want to get a nice folder to put copies of the records in."

Sylvia was nervous on Saturday morning. She'd made copies of everything, and placed them inside the new folder. She made tea, and waited for Mr. Kinsey to arrive.

Somewhere near ten o'clock, he knocked at the door. She looked at the man, trying to find some resemblance to Old Squire. She didn't think he favored him at all.

"Please, come in. You came alone?"

"Yes, I live closer than the other relatives."

"Would you like some tea?"

"No thank you. I'm anxious to hear what you have to say."

"I found information on this land which was once a large plantation. I purchased the property in nineteen sixty four without knowing the complete history."

She showed him the record of land purchase, and letters documenting the plantation's existence.

"Along with these, I found an old Will, written by the plantation owner. It contains several slaves, listed by first names only. Squire is in this will. Now, these documents prove the genealogy line from Squire to you, Mr. Kinsey."

He looked over the papers. He found the names Isaac, Esau, Purcell and his father's name, Walter Kinsey, Sr.. After reading for several minutes, he put the papers aside.

"It appears that these are my family members. Squire and Molly, they were slaves on this land?"

"Yes."

"So, they just took the name Kinsey from the owner?"

"It was a common practice. I guess their ancestors lost their names when they came to this country."

"I guess."

"My ancestors are in that Will too."

"The one signing it, I suppose."

"I'm not proud of the content of that Will. I just wanted to acknowledge that I know what happened to your relatives. I'm saddened by all slavery, and never expected to find a personal accounting of it in my family's background. I can tell you that I've spoken with someone who knows the history here, and they've said that there was no physical abuse. To be held in bondage is bad enough! I just hoped you'd feel better knowing that your ancestors weren't physically abused. I can't change what happened, but I am so sorry that my ancestors participated."

"Thanks for the information. I'll go now, if that's all."

He gathered his papers, put them back into the folder, and shook his head as he walked to the door.

"I know it's a lot to absorb. I can't even imagine how you must feel."

"No, I don't imagine you could. I do appreciate the attempt to apologize. Thank you."

He was off the porch before Sylvia remembered that she hadn't called Squire. She'd been so nervous she'd forgotten when he knocked at the door.

"Wait!" she called out
"Excuse me?"
"There's more to this."

She was going to tell him the whole story and wasn't sure why. She'd been silent for twenty-seven years. Now she would talk about Squire.

"Mr. Kinsey, please sit. You may think I'm crazy when you hear what I have to say. I just know I have to tell you."

"What?"

"Squire is here. On this place, now."
"He's buried here? That's interesting. I'd like to…"
"No. He sort of lives here."
"As in a ghost?"

"That's right. He's been trapped here since eighteen sixty-seven. I know it sounds crazy, but it's true."

"You know lady, you almost had me. What is this, some scam for a news story? Don't you think we've been through enough without someone like you exploiting the issues? Is any of this stuff true, or did you just fill in the names to match your story?"

He waved the folder at her then threw it down on the porch.

"Please, Mr. Kinsey. You have it all wrong. I've kept him a secret for years because I knew no one would believe. I'm not after anything. I only wanted to help him! I wanted him to see his family just once! I swear to you I'm not lying."

"Forget it, Lady!"
"Squire!" she yelled
Old Squire appeared, and saw that she was upset.

167

"What wrong? Who dat man in de yard? He make you cry, Chille?"

As Mr. Kinsey approached his car, he turned to look at Sylvia once more. She could see the anger in his eyes, and knew the meeting had been a mistake.

"He's your grandson, Squire. He wouldn't believe me when I said that you live here."

"Chille, he look jest like Jabo! Go tell em come here! I wants a see em in his face."

Mr. Kinsey backed out of the driveway and was gone. Sylvia picked up the folder, and went to the swing. She knew she'd made a mess of things.

"He had to leave, Squire. Maybe he'll be back again. I'm sorry."

"You sho' foun' my grandson, did'n ya? I glad a see em looking jest like my Jabo. He be back a see us, you don't worry."

Squire talked about the man all day. He believed that Jabo and Levi must have done well for themselves up north, as the man had been so nicely dressed.

"You see dem shiny shoes? Always want me sompin' like dat. He wus looking nice, Chille. Dat shirt wus clean an' had all dem colors on it! Dem boys musta got um good work."

Stephanie was shocked to learn that Sylvia had told the secret.

"I don't think I would've done that. I mean, now that man just thinks you're Looney. He'll go tell his family you are."

"I know, Stephanie. Don't you think I feel bad enough? Squire did get to see him though. He's been talking about him all day."

"Well, it wasn't a complete loss then. Do you have an address in case you ever wanted to send the box?"

"No. I didn't get a number either. I'm just not going to worry about it. I did find out that he has descendants, anyway."

Chapter Forty-Three

Everyone in the clinic had been sick with a virus except Sylvia. She avoided close contact with any of them. Brittany had been out for two days with the worst case.
"If you need more time off, please go back home Brittany. You still look sick." Sylvia said
"I'll be fine. I haven't been sick this morning. I'm just still a little pale."
By two o'clock Sylvia wasn't feeling well. Richard sent her home, fearing she might have the virus.
At home, she put a pillow on the sofa and turned on the television. She found a talk show, and thought she'd see what the topic of the day might be. To her surprise, the guest was talking of spirits, "Who for some reason, become trapped and can't go forward." She turned up the volume and listened intently.
"They can use electricity; like clocks, televisions, electric lights, etc." the guest said
Sylvia thought of how Squire had manipulated both her clock and television in the past.
"Sometimes spirits are drawn to energy surrounding certain people. Not all people can hear them. You can invite them to stay, or help them to leave."
Sylvia ran to the kitchen during a commercial. She returned when she heard the prompt "How to rid your home of spirits". She settled on the sofa, and grabbed her pen and paper. With intensity, she carefully wrote down all of the instructions given.
"If you have no white candles, buy them. There must be only white light in the room. The more candles, the better. Place at least one in front of a mirror so that the light reflects. You must then call to the spirit. Even if you have no

name, call him out. It is your encouragement that will get the spirit through to the other side." the woman said

Sylvia felt a little unnerved after hearing the instructions. She decided that since Stephanie wanted in on everything she'd call her over when the date was chosen to do the "spirit release." The woman continued, after being asked what a person might say to get the spirit to go through.

"Most spirits are confused. They only need assurance that it will be okay to go toward the light. Somehow they feel the light is a danger. You must convince them it isn't."

A lady in the audience must have read Sylvia's mind when she asked "What light? The candles?"

"No. We all have a light when we cross over. The spirit has a light. You're only intensifying the light with candles."

When the show ended, Sylvia read her notes and was confident that she could follow the instructions. Convincing Stephanie might be more difficult.

As the day passed she realized that the virus had taken over. Hardly able to keep anything on her stomach, she drank broth and juice. By morning she was weak, but much better.

Entering the old hardware store was hard. Sylvia hadn't been inside since her father sold the business. A young salesman approached as she entered the door.

"May I help you?"

"No thanks. I grew up in this store. I think I can find what I need."

Everything had changed. The shelves which once held candles and lanterns, now held nails and screws. Her dad had always arranged things for customer convenience. The most needed items were placed near the front so that customers could grab their purchases easily, and return to work. Now the old carpenters would have to make their way to the back of the store for nails and hammers. In the far front corner of the store, she spotted candles. The salesman approached again.

"We have a large assortment of scented, spice filled, and decorative candles."

Sylvia gathered several plain white candles.

"And this time next year you'll still have them. People don't come in here for such. They buy specialty items in the other stores. This has always been a dependable hardware store. I took all of the emergency candles. You might want to re-order. They go pretty fast during the spring storm season."

"We're trying to change the image of this place. When my uncle bought it, it looked like one of those old country stores. We're carrying lots of new items."

"My father kept this business open for so many years by catering to his customers, son! He deliberately left the store nostalgic because the customers liked it that way!"

"I'm sorry. I didn't know Mr. Champion was your father. I didn't mean any harm. He was always nice to me when I was a kid. I'd come in with my grandfather, and he'd joke around with me. Didn't you have a brother that died in Vietnam?"

"Yes. I am sorry for being defensive. It's just that I haven't been in here since my dad sold the place. It's a little sad to see the changes."

The young man rung up her sale, and she left. She never went back into the old store after that day. It no longer held a part of her dad.

Sylvia stopped by Stephanie's to discuss the plan.

"I need your help with Squire."

"What's the problem?"

"Look at these notes I took. I watched a talk show yesterday, and the guest gave these instructions on how to release spirits."

Stephanie looked over the notes, laughing as she read.

"Will this really work? I mean, through the years you've tried several things. What about the gypsy woman? That was pretty wild, but it didn't work!"

"This does make sense. You've heard of people who died, then came back? They all tell of seeing a bright light. Maybe we can convince him to walk through the light."

"We? I don't know, Aunt Sylvia. It all sounds sort of eerie to me."

"You said we'd been through this together, remember?'"

"When are you planning this great escapade?"

"That's why I'm here. I figured we'd pick a date, spend some time saying our good-byes, then light the candles and send him on his way."

"How are you going to handle this? You've been together for so long. It'll be harder than you think."

"I have to think of him. If he can find Molly, then I'll be fine. I'm sure I'll fall apart when he's gone, but I have to do this."

"All right, I'll help you. I warn you though, if I get transported with him, you have to live long enough to help Gerald raise Ariel."

Chapter Forty-Four

October twelfth was chosen as Squire's date of departure. Sylvia had discussed it with him, and he wasn't convinced he'd really leave.

"I tried talking to de Lawd bout me leavin', he ain't took me. Don't figger I'll be goin' till he say. I wait'n' on dat granboy a come back anyhow. I wants a see em one moe time fo' I goes."

"I don't know if he'll ever come back, Squire. You need to think of Molly and your babies. They'll be waiting for you. Molly's been waiting a long time. You can't disappoint them by just sitting around here with some old crazy white lady!"

"You ain't crazy, Chille. Ain't ole neither. You is white doe! I's fine jest sittin' here wid my white frien'. Reckon you right bout Molly wait'n' on me, doe. I'll be leavin' if you gone get me outah here."

When the twelfth arrived, Stephanie came over with a letter she'd written to Squire. She asked Sylvia to read it so she wouldn't cry before he left.

"Dear Old Squire, I don't know if you've ever realized how much you mean to me. You've been like an uncle or grandfather to me. I came to you with my worries and you made me see them differently. Your love and watchful eye for Molly kept her alive longer than most horses. I want you to tell your wife how much we loved you. It's hard to let you go, but you've been here long enough. I love you, Stephanie."

"Thank you Chille. You take care a dat baby an' tell her bout me one day. Guess I care bout you good bit too. I gone tell Molly everthang we done here."

Sylvia asked for a moment alone with Squire. She opened her hand to reveal Molly's ring.

"I don't know if you can take this with you, but I'll lay it right here at your feet. Maybe when you go, it'll go too. You know this is harder than I can say. I've grown to love not only you, but your Molly and your children. I know them well from the stories you've shared through the years. The old porch won't be the same in the evenings without you there. I don't want you worrying about me though. I'll be fine, and I'll come to see you one day. I want you to meet me when I get to glory, and bring Molly. I'll miss you, Old Squire."

Stephanie came back into the room, and they began lighting candles. Three were placed on the mantle in front of the mirror, and ten more around the room. All of the lights were turned off. The room was filled with brilliant white light. Old Squire stood right in front of the mantle, surrounded by a soft, white glow. Sylvia placed Molly's ring at his feet and backed away.

"Old Squire" she said, "Can you see the light?"

"Show can. It all roun' dis room!"

"We want you to go through the light. It won't hurt you." Stephanie told him

"Walk into the light, Squire." urged Stephanie

Old Squire walked forward toward a candle, which sat on the coffee table. He then turned and walked back to the three candles on the mantle. Nothing happened!

"Aunt Sylvia, he's just walking to the candles. He's supposed to see his own white light, isn't he?"

Checking her notes, Sylvia found that Stephanie was correct.

"Old Squire, you need to go through your own white light. Not the candles!"

"Ain't no light cept des cannels, Chille. I ain't got no white light!"

"Let's hold hands and close our eyes, Stephanie. Concentrate on him leaving."

"You're kidding, right?"

"Well, do you have any suggestions?"

They held hands and tried to envision the old man traveling through a white tunnel of light. When they opened their eyes, Old Squire was laughing.

"I sorry. Ya'll tryin' so hard a get rid a me, an' I still jest be standin' here. Cannels reel pertty doe, an' it wus nice hearin' ya'll talk so good bout me."

They burst into laughter and fell on the sofa. Sylvia began blowing out the candles. Stephanie turned on the lights.

"I guess there's a statute of limitations on white tunnel travel." Stephanie laughed "Or perhaps he's used up his frequent flyer miles!"

"That will be enough. So it didn't work, what else is new? I've been trying for over twenty years, and it's just no use. He's destined to remain here."

"We get long pretty good. I jest stay here wid you till Lawd call me. My grandboy comin' back anyhow. Be wrong a leave fo' den."

"I never wanted you to go anyway, Old Squire. We're fine just like we are; you and me and this old house!"

The candles were discarded, and the ring placed back into the box. Stephanie saw the box for the first time.

"This is really amazing! I wonder what it'd be worth?"

"It doesn't matter. I never even thought of the value. It isn't mine to worry about!"

"I know you'd never sell any of this, I was just curious. It's a shame that guy didn't believe you. I'm sure he'd want this stuff. Where did he live?"

"Fairview or Fairfield, South Carolina."

"Why don't you try again?"

"No. It's best left alone. He was really angry when he left that day."

Chapter Forty-Five

The office calendar was marked with important dates for the doctors. Mechelle was in charge of noting all appointments, meetings, and personal reminders. Sylvia checked the calendar on Monday, and noticed a Doctors appointment marked for February twenty-first. Penciled in were the names, Mechelle and Sylvia. She removed the calendar, and went to Mechelle's desk.

"What's this doctor's appointment?"

"Oh, I was going to bring that up. They're holding a "Bring a friend" mammogram screening. I was hoping you'd agree to go. We're both beyond the safe age zone, you know. You haven't had a physical in three years either."

"There's no breast cancer in my family that I'm aware of."

"It starts somewhere doesn't it? I don't think it's always genetic."

"Okay, okay, I'll go!"

Two weeks later they went in for the screening. Mechelle was given no consultation after her screening and was told to call back in five days, after the doctor reviewed the test. Sylvia was called in to talk with a nurse after her screening. The nurse did a physical breast exam and confirmed a mass, seen on the mammogram. She asked that Sylvia make an appointment to see the doctor before leaving. On the ride back to the clinic, Sylvia was silent.

"Don't worry too much" Mechelle said "It's probably one of these fibroadenomas I've been reading about in this literature. They're benign, but can be confused with malignant cyst on a mammogram."

"Let's change the subject. I'd rather not think about it until my next appointment."

Dr. Kendall's office called in two days to discuss the doctor's decision to do a biopsy of the cyst. The procedure would be done in his clinic, five days later.

Upon arrival for the biopsy, a detailed description of what to expect was given by a nurse.

"We'll use a local anesthetic. The procedure is very simple, limited to the suspected area only, and will result in minimal postoperative discomfort. Our facility is well equipped with qualified staff in each area needed, and equipment necessary to perform biopsy's here, versus the hospital, for your convenience. Do you have any questions?"

"No, you've covered everything quite well. It almost sounds like a delightful experience."

She'd chosen not to alarm her mother unnecessarily. Now seventy-one, she'd already lost one child, and her husband. Sylvia thought of her mother during the procedure that day. Her strength, and strong will had always been so evident to those around her. Sylvia hoped she'd find the same strength should the biopsy reveal a malignancy.

The ordeal was over in a few minutes, and a small bandage was applied. After receiving her instruction sheet on care of the small wound, she was asked to make an appointment for seven days later.

"When will I be advised of the results?"

"On your appointment date. The doctor will consult with you at that time."

Sylvia dressed, thanked the nurse, made her appointment, and returned to work. She dreaded the looks she'd get once inside the clinic, the sympathetic "what if she's dying" looks. They'd be overly polite, not wanting to ask the question hanging in the air; "Is it cancer?"

Once inside, she spoke to a client waiting in the lobby.

"What seems to be wrong with Daisy today, Mrs. Johnson?"

"She's throwing up again and won't eat her food."

The poodle was lying across her lap. It seemed too much for the animal to even look up and respond to Sylvia's voice.

"We'll have a look in a moment."

She knew that Mrs. Johnson had a habit of feeding a few bites of tasty roast beef and chicken to the dog. She'd been warned against the practice in the past, but evidently wasn't paying attention.

"Hi, you have a cat in exam three, and Mrs. Johnson is waiting in the lobby." Mechelle said.

"Thanks. I spoke with Mrs. Johnson."

No looks, no comments, no questions, just business as usual. She was relieved, but for a second, somewhat disappointed. Richard hadn't come out to speak to her, and there was no sign of Brittany or Kelly. . Mechelle didn't ask anything! "God, I need to get a grip" she thought, "I didn't want sympathy. Now I'm wondering why I got none."

"Good afternoon, Old Tom. Let's have a look at that foot."

A splinter was removed from the cat's paw, ointment applied, and he'd be fine. Mrs. Johnson was advised not to feed the poodle from the table again. She was given medication to administer four times a day, and sent home with Daisy.

Making notations on her charts, Sylvia thought of how many animals she'd patched up or easily cured over the years. She wished her situation was so simple, but she knew if cancer was found she'd be in for serious treatment.

Before leaving the clinic, all of her coworkers filed into her office to offer a much needed hug. Nothing was said; there was no need. She felt their emotion with each embrace. She refused to cry in front of them. They all looked to her for guidance. Mechelle and Richard had leaned on her like an older sister for over twenty years. She felt she had to show strength to all of them.

"Thank you for the hugs" she said "but I really am quite okay with my inconvenient situation. There may be need for me to be out of the office for a while. I'm counting on each of you to keep things going, and continue as usual. Now, let's go home."

The next few days were torture for Sylvia. She expressed no concern at the clinic, but once home each night she fell apart. Sleeping became a rarity, and talking with Old Squire, not an option. She was sure he heard her crying, and was surprised that he hadn't appeared. She wondered if he somehow knew to leave her alone. She didn't want to discuss it with him. She wasn't sure he'd understand the term "cancer". What he would understand was death. She prayed that discussion wouldn't be necessary.

It was a Friday when she went in for the consultation. Dr. Kendall pulled no punches. His approach was painfully direct.

"You have breast cancer in the left breast. The mass, seen as suspicious on the mammogram and physical examination, came back malignant after the biopsy. This needs to be attacked with immediate, and aggressive treatment."

"What type of treatment?"

"We will do a modified mastectomy, leaving the pectoral muscles intact. This makes reconstructive surgery easier. I will make a determination on whether or not to recommend radiation therapy after surgery. It's sometimes necessary to protect against recurrence."

"What about nausea, hair loss, and reactions?"

"We have some medications which help many patients with nausea. Most, experience hair loss. Reactions can range from mild to severe. I'd like to schedule surgery for next week. Say Wednesday?"

"That soon? I need to talk to my family and make arrangements at my clinic. How long will recovery take?"

"We'll discuss that a few days after surgery. Let's get the important things done first. So, Wednesday then?"

"I suppose. Yes, Wednesday."

"Good. I'll have my office call the hospital and set everything up. They'll call you for pre-admission information."

Dr. Kendall stood up, shook her hand, and promised to be in touch. So routine for him she thought.

There was no conscious memory of leaving the doctor's office or driving home. Sylvia parked the car in the drive, and went into the house. Once inside, she methodically showered, put on her robe, and went to bed. Curling up in a fetal position, she wept from the depths of her soul. For most of the evening she just lay there until she could cry no more. Afterwards, she engaged in some unconscious humming, as she gently rocked back and forth on the bed. For two days, she remained in her bed. Depressed, frightened, and unable to face anyone, she couldn't get up.

Mechelle had called three times, leaving messages each time. The last had been a threat to call Sylvia's mother. That call snapped her back to reality. She didn't want anyone else to tell her mother.

"Hi Mechelle, it's Sylvia. You haven't called Mom have you?"

"You know I wouldn't do that. I had to scare you enough to make you call. I came over there twice, and knocked on the door. Why wouldn't you answer?"

"Honestly, I never heard you. I did hear the answering machine a couple of times, but I just couldn't talk to anyone for a while. I'm sorry I've worried you. I just needed to be alone to feel sorry for myself I guess."

"You are going to tell your mom aren't you? She'd never forgive you if you didn't tell her what's going on."

"I'll call her in a few minutes. I'll arrange to meet her for lunch tomorrow and tell her then. It's not easy hitting her with this. I've gotta talk to Matt and Deborah too. Then there's Stephanie and Jonathan. I hate this Mechelle!"

"Listen to me! You're one of the strongest people I've ever known. You can get through this, but don't shut out people who want to help you. It is treatable, right?"

"Yeah. Surgery and possible radiation."

"This won't get the best of you. We're all praying and believing that."

"I'll be in tomorrow to go over some things. Do you think everyone would come in? I know the girls rotate Saturday's."

"I can guarantee it! Is there something I can do? bring you anything at all?"

"No. Your concern and encouragement are enough. I'm going to go now. I'll see you in the morning."

Sylvia called her mother. She imagined the fact that she'd kept everything secret up to that point wouldn't set well with her.

"Hi Mom. I'm sorry I haven't called in a few days. I've been really busy. Listen, I thought we might meet for lunch tomorrow. We'll go to the seafood place. What do you think?"

"That sounds good to me. Is everything okay with you? I called the office yesterday, and Mechelle said you weren't coming in. Something you had to take care of? I tried the house, and got that answering machine. I can't talk on those things."

"I just needed the day off. I'll meet you at twelve fifteen tomorrow, okay?"

There was never a time she could remember when she'd successfully lied to her mother. Ending the conversation quickly was her only way out. She didn't actually lie she supposed, she just hadn't told the whole story.

The meeting was held the next morning at the clinic. Everyone assured Sylvia that things would go on just as she wished. She left the clinic at twelve to meet her mother.

"You're always so punctual! I figured you'd beat me here." Sylvia said as she approached the table.

"I've been anxious to hear what's going on with you. I know something's wrong, Sylvia."

"Let's get some lunch first. What are you in the mood for?"

"Just salad and tea for me, but you get whatever you want."

Diana picked at her food, and glanced often across the table, trying to get some indication that her fears weren't valid. Finally she demanded an answer.

"Sylvia, you tell me right now what's going on! I can deal with whatever it is, but you have to be honest with me."

"You remember all the band aids you wasted on me when I was a little girl?"

"Lord, I'd guess maybe five thousand or so. Why?"

"You always seemed to fix everything for me. No matter what my problems were, I could come to you and you'd fix them. Mom, it'll take more than a band-aid this time. I have a major problem."

"What is it, Sylvia?"

Sylvia reached across the table, and held her mother's hand.

"It's breast cancer."

She watched as the color drained from her mothers face. Diana quietly wiped a tear with her napkin, and looked toward the window of the restaurant. After a moment, she turned to Sylvia.

"How long have you known? What treatment will you need?"

"It was confirmed last Friday. I'm having surgery on Wednesday, and then we'll go from there."

"Don't ever keep something this important from me again. Being kept in the dark is worse than knowing the truth. I've felt that something was wrong for days!"

"I'm sorry, Mom. I didn't want to upset you. I forget how indestructible you are sometimes. I wish I had that part of you."

"You do! You just haven't had to use it often. Now might be a good time. We'll handle this together. You'll come home with me after surgery, and I'll take care of you."

Talking with Stephanie that afternoon didn't go as well.

"What guarantee do you have that it'll be gone after the surgery?"

"There are no absolutes, Stephanie! This is my best shot. Long-term survival is much more common now. I'm confident, and I need for you to be."

"Have you told Grandma and Daddy?"

"Just Grandma. I had lunch with her today and told her. I'll talk to your dad tonight."

"I love you so much. This isn't fair! I can't even imagine my life without you. We've always been so close."

"And we will be for a long time."

Chapter Forty-Six

Wednesday morning turned into a friend and family reunion. The hospital corridor was lined with people when Sylvia arrived. Matt and his whole family on one side, the clinic staff members along the other. Marty ran to meet her with open arms.

"You thought you'd throw a party and not invite me?"

"Thanks for coming, Sport. It means a lot."

With tears in her eyes, she thanked everyone, and went to check in.

The surgery went well, Dr. Kendall reported later. No radiation therapy would be ordered, he determined, after testing the surrounding tissue, and lymph nodes. Reconstructive surgery would be done later when Sylvia felt well enough. His report brought cheers from the waiting crowd.

Although extremely sore and still groggy, Sylvia was glad it was over. When alert, her mother gave her the good news. She remained in the hospital a few days, but had a steady stream of visitors. Clients even brought cards from their pets. Once released, she felt wonderful. After staying two days with her mother, she wanted to go home.

"I'll be fine, Mom! I'm following the doctor's orders and can manage alone."

"What about the dressing?"

"I can handle it. You've done so much in the past few days. You need to take care of yourself!"

"I'm not going to argue with you. You have your father's stubborn streak! If you need me, you know I'll be here. You can call me anytime day or night. Promise?"

"I promise. You can still come over and fix my breakfast if you want." Sylvia laughed

That afternoon she gathered her things, and went home. No matter what problems she'd faced, the old house always welcomed her home with its warm, friendly face.

"Old Squire, I'm home."

"Chille, I worry an' worry. All dat cryin' you done, den jest up an' wus gone. Did'n' know what a do. Did'n' know if you comin' back."

"I had a problem, and I went to the hospital. I'm better now though. I want to ask you something."

"I hears ya."

"What if I didn't go back to work and was here more? Would you get tired of me?"

"Naw, you jest plum silly sometime. I wants you roun' here a talk to. I got stories you ain't heard yet. We be even better friens' if you here most time."

"Well, I think I'm going to retire from the clinic. I have so much I want to do while I'm still able to do things."

"You got money nuff fo' food? We been here long time gether. You ain't never growed no food, jest dem flowers. Cain't eat dem flowers! You needs a learn a grow food! Tole you a get a man when you wus young girl. Bout too late now!"

"I've saved my money. I'll be fine, and besides, I don't eat that much!"

She laughed at his idea of a helpless woman starving to death. He'd always gone back to the subject of her not having a man to support her. Their worlds were so far apart. More than the years, progress he'd missed. There were such changes in women's rights, minority and civil rights, airplanes, and rapid transit. All took place without his knowledge. It didn't matter in their relationship. Their conversations were never about the outside world, only their own.

Sylvia returned to work before the doctor released her. She was anxious to work out a time for retirement. She agreed to stay on for two months. A new doctor would be needed to fill in the gap she'd leave. Mechelle put the word out to the universities, and hoped to find someone who would fit in. Richard bought Sylvia's interest in the business, but hadn't decided whether or not to take on a partner, versus a salaried doctor.

"I never imagined making these decisions." he said "We've been together so long, I guess I took for granted that we'd retire together. It's hard to think of being here without you, but I'd do the same if I'd faced what you did."

"I'll visit, and we'll always be friends. My situation just made me take a look at life a little differently. I know you guys understand."

It had been two weeks since Mechelle requested applications. She'd heard nothing. Struggling with the door key, she hurried to catch the phone. She hoped it was a potential applicant.

"Good morning, Animal Wellness."

"You're out of breath. Been jogging?"

"Hey Marty. No the darn key stuck again. I was hoping you were an applicant."

"For what?"

"Sylvia's retiring."

"You're kidding me!"

"No, she wants to do other things for a while. It's the cancer thing. I think she's afraid that she might run out of time or something."

"They got all the cancer didn't they?"

"Yeah, but I'm sure it's in the back of her mind."

"Why didn't someone call me?"

"What could you do that we haven't? We've tried talking her out of it, even suggested that she stay on part time, but she's determined to retire."

"I know how she is! Once she decides, there's no changing her mind. I meant about the position."

"You know somebody?"

"Yep. He's nice looking, friendly, has great communication skills with animals, works well with others, and more."

"Send him to us, or have him call. He can fax a resume!"

"Mechelle, you're slipping. Surely you know I'm the only doctor with those qualifications!"

She let out a yell.

"I didn't even think to ask you. I thought you were happy there. Are you serious?"

"Yes, I'm serious!"

"When could you leave your position there?"

"Well, I can come on down and discuss everything, then come back and clear everything here. I'm not a partner here, just salaried."

"Let's not tell Richard or Sylvia. I'll tell them I have an applicant coming in to meet with them. When will you be here?"

"How about Saturday morning?"

"Great! I'll let you go. Be here at eight o'clock."

Mechelle laid it on thick. She described the perfect partner, and was excited for them that they might have their man.

"I'm glad someone finally called. We'll talk to him, but I never believe everything said over the phone. I like to see the person face to face, and then make a decision."

On Friday afternoon, Mechelle confided in Brittany.

"I need for someone to pick up a cake and decorations. Keep them out of sight in the morning until we can figure where to decorate."

"I love this job! There's always something going on behind somebody's back!"

"Just don't mention Marty to anyone here, okay?"

"Is this Marty guy cute?"

"I think he's a little old for you. You have a boyfriend anyway!"

"We had a fuss last night. I'm not sure if I still like him or not."

"Oh the romance of teenagers!"

The clinic opened at seven thirty on Saturday morning. Sylvia was late, and Mechelle panicked at the thought of her running into Marty in the parking lot. She sent Brittany to decorate exam room four.

"Good morning Sylvia. You're a little late. I was getting worried!" Mechelle said

"I'm seven minutes late Mechelle. Get a grip!"

"Richard, you and Sylvia go into her office. That guy will be here any minute for the interview!"

"And the clients?"

"We don't have anything until nine o'clock."

They did as directed, and the two of them waited for the applicant to arrive.

"I made a list of questions. I wanted to be sure I covered everything." Richard said

"That's good. It's always better if you know what questions you intend to ask."

"Do you have a list?"

"No."

Mechelle came to the door.

"Hey. Can ya'll come to exam four?"

"I thought you said we didn't have anything until nine oclock."

"Just came in. Hurry!"

Walking into the exam room, they spotted Marty.

"Heard you were looking for a doctor. I'd like to apply for the position. I come highly recommended!"

"Are you being funny, or is this for real?" asked Richard

"I'm really here about the job! I spoke with Mechelle on Thursday."

"Well that solves my worries about trusting another partner!"

"Marty, this is wonderful!" said Sylvia "I can leave knowing things will go on the same. Welcome home!"

Marty left the next Tuesday to clear up things in South Carolina. He planned to take three weeks off between jobs, but would fall right back into the routine in time for Sylvia's retirement.

Chapter Forty-Seven

The first year of retirement was a whirlwind of activity for Sylvia. She attended her first Auburn Alumni reunion in fifteen years, and spent time with old friends. They planned several trips during the week together. Over the next two years Sylvia toured Canada, Ireland, Mexico, and the Florida keys with her friends. Diana joined the group for the Florida trip, and enjoyed being included with the younger women.

Whenever home, Sylvia and Squire spent hours talking and enjoying the evenings outside. She never tired of his stories. Some were sad, but often he would tell a funny tale of simpler times.

"I gone tell you bout a lazy man. Dat man wus lazier an' any dawg laying up under a shade on a bright sun day. Some reason, dat man's fields did'n' made nuttin'. Cain't member what de reason wus now. Anyhow, he had bout ten little youngins gone go widout food. Massa awder two wagons be loaded wid corn cause Massa corn made good dat year. We loaded dem wagons an' Massa took me, his boys, an Miss Amy go give dat man some corn. We pull up front of de house an' Massa yells "Missa Jon, we brung dis corn fo' yo' family." Well Chille, dat lazy man did'n' rise up off dat chair. Jest sit deah whittlin'. He looks up an' yell "Is it shucked?" Massa holler at dem hawses "Gettiup!" an' we took all dat corn right back here. Unload dem wagons; never talk of it no moc."

"Old Squire, you should've been a story teller. You'd be a rich man today if you were able to write down some of those old tales and sell them." Sylvia said

"Stories all foke got when dey cain't read or write. We's always tole stories roun' back a de cabins, late nights. Only way a know different thangs. Heard me lots a stories back deah, sho' did."

He looked off as if staring into a memory too personal, or perhaps too painful, to share. She wouldn't ask what he was thinking when he was absorbed in thought. She was sure there was many stories she'd never hear, and that was okay.

While visiting the nursing home one afternoon, Sylvia thought of what Old Squire had said about stories being the only means of communicating information. There were many in the home that could no longer read, probably some who never could. She went to the library. After selecting several books, she returned home to sort through the short story volumes, and find interesting tales to read to aloud at the home. She found the idea of taking the elderly people away from their mundane existence for an hour, rewarding. She'd seen the results of the pet visitation program, and felt that reading to some of the patients would have a positive effect too.

The reading program turned out to be an excellent escape for the old people. From reading, came the idea of casting patients into roles of the book characters. Simple plays were put on for visitors on the third Sunday of each month. Sylvia's mom joined the venture, and helped to make the costumes. For those still able to recall their past, Sylvia encouraged a story telling group where they shared wonderful tales of their lives. Squire had influenced their lives without even knowing.

"Old Squire"

"I been out at de barn jest looking roun'."

"You've done a wonderful thing for some old people."

"What I did?"

"You inspired me to start a story telling program! They have groups who tell old tales to each other and some who listen to readers. We even dress them up, and they play parts of the stories. Next month, we're doing a skit about your corn story!"

"Fokes like dat story?"

"They loved it! It's really funny, but also teaches so much about being grateful for things people give you."

"Ole Squire pretty smart now. Ustah be call dumb by some foke. Never bother me none. I knowed I could'n read, but I heard an' watch so's I learn. I glad if my story make dem old fokes happy."

Sylvia ran inside to answer the telephone.

"Aunt Sylvia, I hate to ask on short notice, but I need a babysitter. I've got a meeting, and Gerald isn't home yet!"

"Bring her over here. You know I'd love to keep her. Squire will be so tickled when I tell him. We were out on the porch."

"Are you sure? I hate to impose."

"I said bring her over here! We'll have a good time."

"Guess who's coming to stay for a while, Squire."

"Don't know."

"Ariel! Stephanie is bringing her by."

"Ain't seen dat baby in a while. She growed much?"

"She's two years old, talking up a storm and walking."

"Lawd, babies comin' in de world already done smarter dan' grown fokes ustah be."

Ariel was happy to see her aunt. She loved the old swing, and sang as the chains creaked with each back and forth motion.

"What's that you're singing, Ariel?"

"London bridge."

"I'll bet your mama taught that to you."

"No, Paw Paw."

Sylvia was surprised, and proud to hear that her brother was taking time to teach the silly songs they'd learned as children, to his grandchild.

"Know what?"

"What?"

"I'm two years old! I'm a big girl and I can count."

"Your mama told me. Will you count for me?"

She counted to ten then asked for a penny.

"I'll give you one when we go inside. I don't have any money out here."

Ariel laid her head in Sylvia's lap and dozed off in the swing.

It was late when Gerald arrived to take Ariel home.

"You can just leave her if you want. She can sleep with me tonight. I'll bring her home in the morning."

"I'd better get her to the house. She don't sleep well away from her own bed. Thanks for watching her tonight."

He gathered the little sleeping bundle, and left.

"She's so sweet isn't she Squire?"

"I could jest watch her play all day!"

"I'm going to turn in. I'll see you tomorrow."

"I's goin' to de barn awhile."

"Why do you spend so much time out in the barn?"

"Guess I got thangs a member out deah. When you goes a sleep, thangs too quiet."

Chapter Forty-Eight

Stephanie was frantically waving a newspaper as she entered the door.
"Look on page three, bottom half of the page!"
"What?" Sylvia asked.
"Just look! That child, right there."
She pointed to a child standing by a large trophy. The caption read, "State Jr. Math Champion, 1992- Walter Kinsey III. Sylvia read the article, and found that he was from Fairview, South Carolina.
"He has to be that man's son. Don't you think?"
"I imagine he is. He's evidently a very bright child."
"Let's show it to Squire. I'll read the article to him."
"No! He's stopped asking about Walter. I don't want to open that can of worms again."
"Do you know how hard that competition is? This is really great! From slavery to state champion."
"Can you, being a teacher, find out how well he does in other subjects? I'd like to know what his chances of getting into medical school might be. The article states that his parents hope he'll become a doctor. That's an awful lot of tuition. Hopefully he'll keep his grades up, and can get scholarships. Look, it says his father is a firefighter and his mother works in manufacturing."
"I can try to find out for you, but they are in another state. We're talking like we're really kin to this kid. It's a shame we can't find a descendant who'd believe you. It's such a rich heritage. Even with the struggle and pain of it, most of them have no idea who they're ancestors were. We have information on this family, and they don't want it."
Sylvia began writing that evening. "Memories of the slave, Squire Kinsey" was written on the front of the journal.

She wrote for a week, telling of how she met Squire, how he'd been on the place for so many years, and all about his life as a slave and as a ghost. She recanted his stories of family and of the horse, Molly. She was hopeful that someone would be interested one day.

Stephanie was able to find that the child was in a gifted children's program, and was excelling in all subjects. He was ahead of most children his age.

"If he continues this way, I see promise of scholarships, Aunt Sylvia. Why are you so interested in him?"

"His father didn't believe me. I thought that this child might believe one day. I guess since he may become a doctor, and I'm a veterinarian, he might not think I was crazy. I want the box to go to someone. If not his father, maybe to him."

"You're already planning on how to disperse things? What about Squire? What are your plans for him?"

"You know I don't have any control over him. I don't even want to think about him walking around here for another hundred years. I thought maybe if I had the house and the barn torn down before I die, it might free him."

"I don't think so! He was here before the house or the barn. He's trapped on this land, not the structures! I guess I could come by and talk to him until the new owners call the police to me!" she laughed

"I hadn't thought of that! I could leave this place to you, then you could visit anytime."

"And when I die? I guess I'm supposed to find another solution?"

"I guess."

"I need to go. I've got to get a casserole in the oven by five o'clock. Why don't you come eat with us?"

"I appreciate the offer, but I need to clean out my junk drawer. It was so full of paper yesterday, I had to use a spatula to hold the paper while I opened the drawer."

"Offer's always open, you know."

Chapter Forty-Nine

Determined to prove once and for all that she could grow vegetables, Sylvia hired a contractor to prepare the ground for a garden spot, in the spring of nineteen ninety-four. When the grass and a top layer of clay were removed, she ordered several loads of topsoil. Purchase of gardening magazines was a must. She decided on three, and read articles on what to add to the soil, how to fertilize, planting vine plants, and the best tomatoes. With gardening tools in hand, she was ready to begin!

Spreading topsoil from the mountains left by the dump trucks proved a bit more than imagined. She shoveled for two days, knowing Squire was watching to see if she'd give up. Once the ground was leveled, she referred to the articles. Reading about vine type plants, she realized that hills would be necessary. After reshaping the area, she planted squash, cucumber, and melon seeds. On the flat areas, she dropped seed for butter beans, okra, purple hull peas, and corn. The last plantings were tomatoes. Already small plants, they were easily added. When the sun disappeared that afternoon, she was covered with black dirt, but proud of her accomplishment.

Each morning Sylvia checked for anything coming through the soil. She followed all instructions, and waited patiently. She'd wait until everything appeared to be living to talk to Squire. She knew he'd been watching, but dreaded hearing his comments if nothing came up. Finally everything sprouted at once. Now, she could brag!

"Squire?"

"Yep"

"Have you seen the garden?"

"Sho' have. You doin' a fine job! Fo' long you gone have so much food, you haffa give some way."
"See, I don't need a man after all!"
"Reckon ya don't Chille."
As spring turned to summer, the garden flourished. There were more squash and cucumbers than expected. Weekly spraying with pesticides kept insects at bay. New recipes were found for interesting squash dishes. Sylvia's favorite was squash dressing, which tasted like chicken and dressing without the added fat. She gave away surplus squash and cucumbers, making a delivery by the clinic each week with a large basket. The butter beans came next, and had she known how low to the ground they grew, she wouldn't have planted them! Sylvia met an old lady in the grocery store who was checking prices on beans. She advised that sitting on a five gallon bucket while picking butter beans would save the back!
"Don't pay that high price for those beans! You've taught me something today, so I'll bring you some of mine." Sylvia said
"They are mighty high in the stores ain't they?"
She made note of the woman's address and did take her some vegetables each time she harvested. "How sad" she thought "that others who have extra in their gardens can't spare a little to share with the elderly." She learned that the woman, who had no family near by, walked to the store each week, and lived on social security.
"Some months, it just don't go far enough. I have my rent and utilities to pay, and I'm scared to go without my phone. I do okay I guess. Some of my neighbors share meals sometimes. We're all old ladies in the same fix. You're so sweet to bring these things to me, but you have to let me do something for you. I ain't got money, but I can make you something! You like banana puddin'? I make the best in the county!"
"It's my favorite! I haven't had any since my grandmother died."

Sylvia thought of the ingredients needed to make the pudding. She estimated the cost, and worried that the woman would go without something just to make her dessert. She knew it was a matter of pride to the woman, and decided to just accept the offer.

Learning which day the woman walked to the store, Sylvia appeared on her doorstep that day each week. Soon, she was taking all of the old ladies to pay their bills, mail letters, and shop for groceries. She shared conversation, and occasionally a meal with them. They weren't so different from Old Squire, she thought.

The garden turned into a wonderful experience. Sylvia was able to meet so many new friends, and learned about the wonders of giving. Her grandmother had always said: "you start out giving to help other folks, and end up helping yourself more." She hadn't understood that as a child. Through the years, she'd found it to be the truth.

One afternoon, while holding a pea shelling with the old ladies, the subject of spirits came up. She listened as she heard old tales of ghost being trapped in old houses, and of people who just lived around them.

"They never hurt nobody, they just want some company." Miss Emily said, "Papa always told us to ignore them, and they'd leave us alone. Some nights we'd see a woman just floatin' across the bedroom. She had a long dress on, and her feet didn't touch the floor. We'd cover our heads with the quilt, and she'd leave!"

"Did she ever speak to you?" Sylvia asked

"No. I don't think ghost can talk to you, Honey."

Sylvia enjoyed the stories. She couldn't talk about Squire, but hearing other's experiences was nice. She didn't feel so unusual.

"Miss Mary, why don't people believe in ghost anymore? If you speak of them, people think you're crazy!"

"Honey, ghosts were left in the old houses where they'd lived and died. Now days people don't stay in one house long enough to have no history. That's what I think. Young folks buy houses with no history then they move around all their lives. Folks used to stay put!"

That made sense, Sylvia reasoned. She grew to love the old women. Miss Mary had been the first she met, then Miss Emily, Miss Sally, and Miss Kate. They preferred to be called by their first names. Miss Emily had said it made them feel younger!

When winter arrived in ninety-four, the group of women surprised Sylvia with a quilt they'd pieced together from special squares of their materials. She learned the pattern was called "log cabin", and thought it to be the most beautiful thing she'd ever received. No machine work had been done at all; everything stitched by hand.

"I don't know what to do with you girls! You should sell this, and make yourselves a little money."

"We wanted you to have it. It has a part of each of us sewn in. You've been so sweet, and gave us all those nice vegetables. It's the least we can do for you." said Miss Kate.

Miss Emily walked slowly to Sylvia's side. She leaned over and whispered, "The squares with the best stitchin' are mine. I do better at stitchin' than the others, but don't tell them I said so."

Sylvia patted her on the shoulder, and nodded. Later she inspected the squares and could find no remarkable difference in any of the stitches!

When Christmas approached, Sylvia put one hundred dollars in four envelopes for the women. She took them shopping for their grandchildren's gifts, paid postage to mail them, and treated everyone to a nice lunch at the downtown diner.

"I found out you've already paid your utilities for December, so I've paid everyone's bills for next month! I've learned so much from all of you. You've shared your meals, your stories, and your friendship with me. Merry Christmas to each of you!"

"Sylvia, you're gone make us cry right here in this restaurant!" Miss Kate said

The ladies had enriched her life, as had the patients at the home. She was happy she'd retired and found so much to do in place of work. At least one day each week was spent with her mother, working on the nursing home plays. It seemed strange that her mother and some of her friends were the same age, but totally different. She had family, and activities. She'd never know the fear of going without groceries before the end of the month. Sylvia was glad that she wouldn't. She never talked about Miss Mary and the other ladies with her mother. She wasn't sure why. She just felt that her mother wouldn't understand the relationship.

Sylvia continued with her nursing home projects, and eventually expanded to include resident's family members. Many had believed that they'd lost the chance to participate in their loved ones lives until volunteering with the program. They were seeing a renewed vitality in their family members.

In nineteen ninety-five Sylvia convinced the housing authority to allow dogs to be placed on the property. Therapeutic and safety values were selling points. She purchased fencing and kennels, and had them placed behind the ladies apartment building. Each was given a leash, and would alternate time spent with the two shelties delivered. Sylvia hoped the dogs would help protect as well as provide stimulation, and keep the ladies independent for many years.

Old Squire loved to hear the old lady stories. He found them most entertaining. Sylvia told him of the dogs she'd delivered to the ladies.

"Ole Squire don't like no dawgs!"

"Why not? They're wonderful companions for people who have no one."

"Recon dey ain't! Miz Cotton had her a dawg. He so mean a me. I want a kill em but I could'n' do nuttin'!"

"The dog could see you?"

"Sho'! All dawgs sees me. Dey come in de yard an' chase me some days. Miz Cotton dawg... he chase an' bark an' growls; tryin' a scare me plum dead! I had a get on de barn or up a tree or sompin'! Don't like no dawg! No dawg!"

She realized that the old horse did see Squire. Stephanie had thought she might have, but they'd never asked Old Squire.

"The dogs I gave to the old ladies are very gentle. They'll be good pets for them, like Molly was a good horse for you."

"Hawses an' dawgs ain't de same!"

Life was good, and Sylvia was content with the path she walked each day. She couldn't have known how drastically things would change, however, within one year.

Chapter Fifty

Sylvia remembered feeling soreness in her chest sometime in February, she told Dr. Kendall.

"It wasn't bad, and it went away the next morning so I didn't become alarmed. Wednesday, it began hurting again."

"When did you first notice a discharge?"

"Last Tuesday. I called and made an appointment when I first saw it. You don't think the cancer has come back, do you?"

"Get up on the table, and lay back. I'll have a look."

His silence frightened her. She tried to see a look that would suggest one way or the other what his opinion was. She saw nothing.

"You never had the reconstructive surgery. Any reason?"

"I'd been through so much at the time, it just wasn't that important to me. I chose prosthesis."

She wondered if perhaps he should've ordered the radiation six years earlier. Maybe he thought the same.

"Have you noticed any pain here, in the area where the breast was removed?"

He pressed firmly on her scarred chest.

"Ouch! That hurts! I thought you understood that the pain was on that side."

"Hummm, the pain is on this side, but you have discharge on the other?"

"Yes."

She heard very little of what he said after that. When finished, she dressed, and returned to where he sat writing. He stood, and walked her to the outer hallway.

"You should schedule another appointment for a mammogram."

She left his office, but made no appointment. She had to decide what to do. More test, surgery, possible radiation. She couldn't take it. It had only been six years! It wasn't fair, not when her life was full, and so many people depended on her, she thought.

Sylvia packed her bags, and left to spend a week in the mountains. She needed the silence to make a decision. The serenity of the north Georgia mountains was wonderful. She walked the trails that afternoon, then settled in to read a book. Trying not to think of what might be growing inside her body, she took a cold tablet, and went to sleep early.

The snow was falling when Sylvia woke up the next morning. White rainfall it seemed, floating gracefully through the air toward the ground. She hadn't seen snow in several years. On the spur of the moment, she grabbed an old cardboard box from a closet, cut it open, and headed outside. She walked up the snow-covered hill behind the bungalow, and placed the cardboard sled on the snow. Down the hill she flew, laughing loudly! She continued to ride that hill until the cardboard became too wet, and fell apart. Walking back to the bungalow, she suddenly felt silly. "How childish that was!" she said aloud.

She lit the fireplace, made coffee, and settled for a frozen dinner, as the road was impassable. There was complete silence, and she loved it. No telephone, no television, just the snow, a fireplace, and the thoughts she tried to avoid.

After six days, Sylvia made her decision. She'd call a family meeting after returning home, to tell them. No secrets…just the truth. She knew they would go through anything with her, and she'd never be completely alone. They might not agree with her choices, but they would be there.

The snow was melting from the roadway as she made her way down the mountain. The Georgia pines in the distance were still heavy laden with white powder. The young limbs were sagging from the extra weight. Going to the mountains had been a good idea. The beauty and solitude had allowed her the freedom to think. Reaching the bottom of the mountain, Sylvia stepped out of the car and took one last look at the winter wonderland above, before heading home.

Sylvia noticed a note on her door as she approached her porch.

"Call the minute you arrive!! Emergency!! Stephanie"

She ran in and called. No answer. She tried her mother and got no answer there either. Thinking of the clinic, she called Mechelle.

"Where have you been? Everyone has been looking for you for three days! How could you just take off without telling someone where you'd be?"

"What's wrong Mechelle?"

"I'm sorry. It's your mom. She's in the hospital. A stroke, I think."

Sylvia threw the telephone against the wall, and ran out. "I should've been there, should've told someone where I'd be!" she said over and over as she drove to the hospital. She hurriedly parked the car, and ran into the hospital lobby.

"I'm looking for Diana Champion!" she yelled

"ICU, fourth floor." the desk clerk said

She stepped off the elevator and ran through the unit, looking into each room. A nurse called out to her.

"Who are you looking for?"

"Diana Champion"

"Second door on the left."

There were tubes and machines connected to her mother. Deborah turned to see Sylvia enter and offered a hug.

"We tried to find you. Are you okay?"

"I'll talk about that later. How bad is she?"

"We aren't sure. She's been out of it mostly. The doctor says she sustained brain damage, and most likely some paralysis. We don't know yet. Her speech is pretty bad. It's hard to understand what she's saying. She hasn't even tried since yesterday."

"Was she home alone?"

"No. She was over at Stephanie's when it happened."

"Mom, its Sylvia. Can you hear me, Mom? This color is terrible for you. I'll have to see if they have something in a nice fuscia for you! Please open your eyes, Mom. You'll be fine, and you'll come home with me. Mom? Open your eyes!"

She laid her head on the bed railing, and began to cry.

"Schilva?"

"It's me, Mom."

"I waaaded for you."

Her speech was slurred, but Sylvia leaned close and managed to make out what was being said.

"I'm so tired, baby. I love everyone; you tell them that. I'm going to see Daddy and David. Say good-bye. Say good-bye, Sylvia!"

"Oh my god Mom! You've been holding on so I'd have a chance to say good-bye. You remembered what I said about Daddy and David. I'm so sorry I wasn't here for you, Mom. I love you so much. You go now, it's okay. Good-bye my Mama. Walk toward the light. They'll be waiting on the other side. Go ahead, it's okay."

The machine alarm went off. Deborah screamed for a nurse, but Diana was gone. Sylvia sat holding her hands and crying. Matt came into the room and saw that his mother had died.

"So, you decided to show up? A little late don't you think?"

"Matt, don't!" Deborah said "She talked with Mom, and everything was fine between them. That's all that matters."

Sylvia ran from the room crying. She went home and locked her doors. She knew that Matt would come over later. She didn't want to deal with him. She couldn't tell where she'd been. Not then.

Stephanie and Deborah arrived alone.

"I'm so sorry about Matt's outburst." Deborah said

"Daddy shouldn't have said what he did, Aunt Sylvia." Stephanie added

"I would've been angry with him if he'd been missing and I couldn't locate him. He's hurting right now. I understand. Stephanie, I'm so glad she was with you when it happened."

"Aunt Sylvia, where were you? It's not like you to take off without a word."

"I know honey, but now isn't the time. We need to go over to Mom's and get her paperwork. She arranged everything when Daddy died so we wouldn't be bothered with details. You know Mom! Anyway, we need her funeral papers, and the insurance policy."

They found the papers neatly filed in a box marked "funeral papers". Deborah offered to take them by the funeral home and then meet them later. Sylvia walked over to Jeremy and Lisa's house. They'd been such good friends to the Champion family. Lisa was overcome with grief.

"It was so sudden, Sylvia. Last weekend she was fine. We talked about how cold it was, and what we planned to do with our yards in the spring. I'm so sorry, honey. How's Matt taking it?"

"Not too well right now. I need to get back to the house with Stephanie. Thanks for always being there for Mom. You must know how much your friendship meant to her. We'll call with the arrangements when we have things settled."

"I loved your Mom. I'll miss her so much. Please let me know where the family will be. I'll tell the church where to take the food."

Matt was parked in the driveway when Sylvia pulled in. He stepped out of his car and approached her.

"Sis, I'm sorry for the way I acted. I just don't understand. Where did you go?"

"I can't discuss it right now. I understand that you're angry with me, honestly I do. We'll talk when everything is over."

The funeral arrangements were carried out the way Diana wanted. "One more funeral we've gone through" Sylvia told Stephanie "It seems we're always burying someone."

As constant as the morning sun, Squire was there to help his friend through another loss.

"Yo' mama wus good. She learn you thangs nobody else did. Learn us bout fokes dyin'. She wid yo' daddy, Chille. He see bout her now."

"I know, it's easier knowing that. I'll miss so many things about her; her laugh, her strength, and even her worrying. She could handle anything! She always seemed to stay calm through the storms."

"She learn you dat too, Chille. You hannels thangs."

"That's funny. She said the same thing to me recently. I've never seen it myself."

Chapter Fifty-One

Diana's Will stated that the estate was to be equally divided between Sylvia and Matt. The property was put up for sale two weeks after the funeral. Personal items were given to Stephanie and Jonathan, which would be keepsakes of their grandparents. All other things would remain in the house until it sold.

Everything settled, no more excuses, Sylvia realized. She had to talk to the family about her health. She started with Stephanie.

"Hey, I need a favor. Could you call your folks and ask them to come over Saturday? Ask that they bring Jonathan too. We need to have a family meeting, of sorts."

"What about? The estate or the money division?"

"Of course not! I wouldn't want anything more, Stephanie."

"Then what is it? You've been acting strange since you came up missing that week."

"I'll discuss everything with everyone together. Will you call for me?"

"Sure."

She had just lay down, when the telephone rang. Assuming it to be Matt with impending questions, she dreaded answering.

"Sylvia, it's Kate. Mary fell and her hip is broke. The ambulance took her away. We called her son in Florida, but he won't come until tomorrow. She don't have nobody up there with her. Could you come take us? We'll give you some gas money. We just know she's scared by herself."

"I'll be right there. Don't even try to pay for gas, you know better!"

Sylvia threw on some clothes, and drove to pick up the three ladies. She helped them out of the car and into the emergency room. Miss Mary was in surgery, the information clerk said. They waited until she was put into a private room, and Sylvia could speak to the doctor.

"Will she be okay?" Sylvia asked

"She'll be fine. It wasn't as bad as some I've seen at her age. The bone didn't shatter. It was a clean break. She'll need help until she's healed. We've put her in a cast. Are you family?"

"No, just her friend. Her son's coming from Florida tomorrow. Thank you for everything you've done. She's a special person."

She went in to see Miss Mary. It was such a sad sight, all the old ladies standing by her bed with such concern on their faces. They'd formed a strong bond living so close to each other.

"We'll take turns staying with her. She needs somebody here with her." said Miss Emily

The nurse came in to check vital signs.

"She won't completely wake up for some time. Why don't some of you get some rest?"

"I'll take everyone else home, and pick you up in the morning, Miss Emily." said Sylvia

"When she wakes up, you tell her all of us was here!" Miss Sally added

"I will."

The next morning brought more bad news. Miss Mary's son saw no choice but to place his mother in a home.

"The housing authority has rules. She can't stay with one of you. You only have one bedroom, just like her. I can't stay, and she's never gotten along well with my wife. Taking her home with me is out of the question. I've made some calls, and it's all arranged." he said

Miss Emily patted Miss Mary's hand throughout the conversation as she cried.

"Don't put me in no home, Son. They don't treat folks real good sometimes in those places. I know, I used to go see my friend over there."

"Mother, I have no other choice! Maybe you'll get better and can go back home soon."

"You just don't want me to come stay with you! I'm scared to go in a home, Carl."

He said nothing.

"She can stay with me in my home until she's back on her feet." Sylvia offered. "I'm a veterinarian, so I do have medical training. It won't cost you anything."

"No. Thank you, but she needs constant medical attention only a home can provide."

Miss Sally went into the hall, and Sylvia joined her.

"Can't you do something? She's always said she didn't want no part of no home."

"I work with the home here in town. I'll talk with them and make sure she gets good care."

Sylvia went back in to speak to Carl.

"She's going to Meadowcare, right?"

"No openings there. She'll be going to Augusta. It's the nearest one available. They said on the phone that it's very nice. I've arranged for transportation next Thursday. The doctor thinks she'll be able to travel by then. I have to get back to Jacksonville. "

After a quick good-bye to his mother, he left.

Sylvia took the ladies home, leaving Miss Sally with Miss Mary. She promised to check on the home in Augusta.

Talking with Old Squire that evening, she brought up the days events, and Miss Mary's situation.

"Why her boy won't care bout her? She autah be stayin' wid em. How bout her friens'?"

"The place where they live has rules about more than one person staying in the apartments. Her son don't want the responsibility, and old people just don't have much say in anything!"

"She can stay wid us! We got plenty room, Chille. We take her!"

"Her son said no. I tried. He wants her put in a nursing home and he's family! I'm just her friend. He won't listen to me. I can't fight for her rights, no one would go against her son's wishes."

Sylvia thought of the television program about four women who lived together and shared expenses. Squire was right! If Miss Mary wanted to live with her friends, she should've been allowed to! If they could find a place, she thought she might help with the expenses and a nurse until Miss Mary was better. She decided that she'd begin searching the next day.

Sylvia had a dream after falling to sleep which would solve Miss Mary's problem. In the dream, she could see Miss Mary trying to break out of a locked room. The window of the room was covered with bars, and she was unable to get through them. It was as if Sylvia was standing inside the room behind Miss Mary and could see out the blocked window. In the distance there was a heavy fog, which moved slowly from left to right. As she strained to see through the fog, she saw a house. The fog slowly began to rise, and the house was revealed. Sylvia realized it was her parent's home! She was awakened by the dream, and called to Squire.

"You awrite?"

"I'm great! I'm going to buy my brother's half of Mom and Dad's house and give it to the old ladies. They can live together after all!"

"You is?"

"Yeah. I've gotta call Matt!"

She quickly grabbed the telephone by the bed, and dialed his number.

"Hello" Matt said groggily

"Matt, it's Sylvia."

"Do you realize what time it is? Two o'clock! Is something wrong?"

"There's nothing wrong, but this was important. Sorry I disturbed your sleep though."

"Well, what is it?"

"I want to buy your part of Mom and Dad's house."

"You moving? I thought you'd never leave that old place. It's okay with me if that's what you want. Is that what the meeting's about?"

"No, and that's been postponed for now. Tell the others, okay? Call the realty company in the morning. I'll get you a check."

"I'll talk to you tomorrow. I'm going back to sleep now." he said

The next morning Sylvia left a message for Stephanie about the meeting, and that she needed help clearing out some things from her parent's home.

It took a few days to work out details concerning Miss Mary. Her son did agree, if the house was approved by an inspector and would cost him nothing! Those things taken care of, Sylvia paid Matt for the house and all contents. There was nice furniture in the house, and she decided to give it to the ladies as well. Stephanie helped to clear out any personal items and rearrange the house so there were four bedrooms.

"I can't believe you're doing this for them, Aunt Sylvia. I mean it's nice of you, but the house might have brought a lot more on the market. You could've cleared enough after paying Dad, to buy them a reasonable place, and still have some money left!"

"Stephanie, it's not about money. You'd have to know these ladies. They have no one to help, and their friend is in trouble. You should've seen Miss Mary begging her son not to put her in a home. You would've done the same thing! The volunteer work I've done since I retired has been the most rewarding of my life. Don't be like your grandmother! She looks through people, never sees their problems as she walks past. Stop and look into the faces, hear the stories, and if you can help…then help!"

"I'm sorry. I didn't mean to make you mad. I really do admire what you're doing. I'll be happy to meet them, and maybe I can bring Ariel sometimes. All old ladies like little kids, don't they?"

"I'm sure these would."

By Monday morning, everything was ready. Sylvia picked up the three ladies, and drove them to the house. She presented the keys when they arrived, and gave them a tour.

"Welcome home! This is all yours. It's paid for, stocked with groceries, and fully furnished. A nurse has been hired for six weeks, to help Miss Mary. Your old things will be moved here by Thursday."

"Honey, you're kiddin' us! Nobody would do this. You paid for us a house? How in the world will we ever pay you back?" Miss Emily asked

Sylvia looked around the room as they laughed, cried, and enjoyed so much excitement together.

"Seeing all of you happy is pay enough. This was my parent's home. They left it to me, so it cost nothing. I have my own house, and didn't want to sell this to strangers. When Miss Mary broke down the other day, I felt so bad for her. This solution came to me, and here we are! Now, I figure the utilities split four ways will be less than what you paid in rent and four telephone bills. Now you can share expenses and your lives!

On Thursday, Miss Mary was surprised! No one told her until the ambulance pulled into the driveway. She thought she was headed for Augusta. It was a heartfelt moment as Sylvia helped her settle into what had once been her own bedroom. The ladies things were packed and delivered. Their old furniture was donated to needy families in the area. The dogs and all of their things were brought over by Marty and Richard.

As Sylvia walked through the kitchen to leave that day, she stopped at the door and turned around. "Mom?" she called "No answer. That's good."

"Spreading the joy of helping those old ladies will bring blessings for the helpers." she told Old Squire

"It jest a good thang ya'll done fo' dem ole women. Wus dey happy a be home? Dat's what I wants, Chille. Be happy when I's home wid my Molly. Reckon we gone have nice place in glory?"

Once again she felt sad for him. He couldn't know how much she wished she could present his family with the finest home money could buy. She couldn't even buy him passage from her house to heaven! Her heart had grown with simple caring, appreciation for the little things in life, and genuine acts of kindness for mankind, because of him. Still she could give him nothing.

"I reckon you will, Old Squire."

Chapter Fifty-Two

Stephanie arrived for the family meeting, before her parents. She felt something was terribly wrong, and feared what Sylvia would tell them. Walking into the front room, she smelled apple pie.

"Aunt Sylvia, I'm here."

"In the kitchen."

The kitchen had always been an inviting room for Stephanie. She stood in the doorway remembering crisp winter mornings, and hot chocolate.

"What? You look like you thought of something good. Want to share?" Sylvia asked

"No. Just thinking of times spent here. Apple pie? I haven't had homemade apple pie in a long time."

"I've got something to give you later. Remind me before you leave."

"What is it?"

"I typed up some of Grandma Champion's recipes for you, so someone will pass them on."

"Thank you. Did you remember the dressing? I never get it right!"

"It's in there! You can look it over and see if I missed anything important. That's your dad at the door. Can you let him in?"

With everyone seated in the front room, Sylvia explained that she'd made a decision, and needed to discuss it.

"Before I begin, let me make it very clear that my decision is final, and it was mine to make! I love each of you and will appreciate you supporting my choices. Please don't try to change my mind after I tell you what my plans are."

"If you've made a crazy decision I'll have to voice my opinion, Sis. That's just me!"

"Matt, try and understand. I'm responsible for me, have been for many years now. At fifty-eight years old I don't need your opinion. I would like to have your support!"

Sylvia drank her coffee, and sat the cup down. Everyone was waiting, anticipating a decision to sell out and leave town, or join some humanitarian venture as a veterinary aide.

"I had a doctor's appointment the day I left for the mountains. I didn't tell anyone about it. I have some symptoms, which are good indications the cancer has returned. I was upset that day and needed to think, so I just ran! I know I upset everyone when Mom had the stroke and no one could find me. For that, I apologize. I just needed to make a decision about my life, and to be alone."

"Aunt Sylvia."

"Please, let me finish! When Mom died, I put off saying anything. We had enough to deal with. I've only had six years since the last surgery. It was a major ordeal for me back then, but I got through it. I don't want to go through it again just to have another five or six years. I've done a lot of praying, thinking, and reading. If it's invaded other areas, as indicated by the symptoms, I'd rather live out my life the best I can for as long as I can. If it becomes painful, I choose to take medication instead of having surgery, chemo, or radiation. The pain wouldn't be worse than the sickness and weakness after treatments, not for me anyway. I've had a pretty good life up till now, and I plan to stay a while longer. However, I choose to stay with dignity! I hope you will understand."

There was silence in the room except for Stephanie's crying. After a moment, Matt spoke.

"First, I owe you a big apology! I had no idea what you were going through when you came to see Mom at the hospital. I'm really sorry for that scene."

"It's okay. I understood all that."

"I think your decision has been made without really considering the consequences. You're choosing death versus life! You've made some strange decisions lately, Sis. I wonder if you're thinking clearly."

"What does that mean, Matt?"

"Well, the house for one! I wouldn't have sold my interest if I'd known what you planned to do. We could've made a hefty profit on the place!"

"I personally made quite a return on my investment, but you'd never understand that kind of bottom line! You want more money, Matt? I'll give you more money! As for insinuating that I'm not capable of making sound judgments about my personal life, it's none of your business! I know what I want, and I'll do only what I want! I wish you could understand that."

There. She'd finally raised her voice to Matt! He didn't look around the room, as if he feared the others were laughing at his being told off by his sister.

"How long will you live without the treatment?"

"I have no idea, and I don't want to know. I didn't have any test run after the doctor did the physical exam. I choose not to know what lies ahead."

"Sylvia" Deborah said, "I do understand. If I were in your shoes, I think I'd make the same decision. It was so bad last time, worrying after each test, waiting for the results, then hoping it was gone. I can agree with your decision."

"Thank you, Deb."

"Aunt Sylvia, I'm trying to understand. Really, I am. I just love you so much, and I don't want Ariel to grow up without you here. You've been such an influence on me, and I wanted her to know you like I did. If this is what you want however, I'll try to support you and learn to accept it."

"Steph, you know I love you and Ariel. I'm not guaranteed that I'd live to see her grown, without having cancer. I plan to spend lots of time with her. She's old enough to remember me."

"I accept your choices, Aunt Sylvia." said Jonathan "As for what you did with Grandma's house, I think it's great! I haven't told anyone, but I've been helping some kids at the boys club. They needed uniforms and shoes, but couldn't afford them. Their smiles and hugs have meant more to me than all the money I've invested in them. I guess we're more alike than I realized!"

Matt said nothing more. She didn't think he would. It was okay; they'd never seen things the same way. She loved him and felt she needed to be honest with him. If he couldn't accept the choices she'd made, it wouldn't change anything.

Two weeks after the meeting, Sylvia called Jonathan to ask if he would take care of her finances.

"If you have a problem with taking it from your father, I'll understand."

"You know I don't care about that. Just take your accounts back, then we'll get together. He doesn't have to know right away what you're doing with them. You don't think Dad would take your money, do you?"

"No. I just have some plans for some of it that he wouldn't agree with. I feel you'd honor my wishes."

With the financial question answered, she felt better. Jonathan had grown into a good man. He possessed some of his dad's ambitious qualities, but had genuine heart, too. That side of him, Sylvia knew, would make his life rewarding.

A written request was sent to Matt concerning the financial portfolio. Sylvia asked that everything be transferred to her bank after talking with Mr. Thornton. He agreed to accept the transfer, and to handle things until she secured another investment firm. By using her bank as the middleman, she could take the pressure off of Jonathan. Surprisingly Matt didn't argue with her. He even called to advise that the transfer had been handled, and asked how she was doing.

Jonathan met with Sylvia, to go over everything. He advised her to make a Will, in case anything did happen to her, while no one could say she wasn't of sound mind enough to make decisions.

"Make everything very clear, Aunt Sylvia. I'm talking right down to the forks and spoons! You don't have children, so everything is estate unless you itemize your disbursements."

So much for her to understand, stocks, bonds, funds, property-real and personal, and special request for certain things to be handled. Sylvia confided in her attorney and gained knowledge of how to word her final wishes. She appointed Stephanie executor of the Will, then made notes of what she wanted each person to have after her death.

To my niece, Stephanie: One third of all stocks and bonds. All household furniture except my personal bedroom suite, all other personal items in my home, and fifty thousand dollars.

To my brother, Matt: Painting of Marine standing at Ferry Landing and wedding ring set which belonged to our parents.

To my nephew, Jonathan: My father's pocket watch, coin collection, and fifty thousand dollars.

To my niece, Ariel: Twenty-five thousand dollars in trust to be available when she reaches nineteen years of age.

To my dear friends, Mechelle and Richard: My personal bedroom suite, and one half ownership of the building and property now known as Animal Wellness Clinic location.

To my dear friend Marty: One half ownership of the building and property now known as Animal Wellness Clinic location, and two thousand dollars.

To my dear friends, Miss Emily, Miss Mary, Miss Sally, and Miss Kate: I leave the total sum of my IRA to be placed into a fund for payment of all monthly household expenses, lawn care, household repairs, and emergencies of the above named persons as long as any one of the above named persons are living. In the event of all persons above becoming deceased, any remaining money is to be donated to Meadowcare Home to be used for patient social activity programs.

To Walter Kinsey Jr., descendant of Squire Kinsey: I leave my property located on highway eleven, and all structures thereon. Squire was a slave on this land in the eighteen hundreds. He remained on this land after being freed, working for shelter and food only, until eighteen sixty-seven when a tornado struck, killing his wife and destroying all original structures. He enjoyed only a few years of freedom during his entire life of some seventy years. His descendants, namely Walter Kinsey Jr. and family, shall inherit a portion of what he and his family knew as home (without choice until eighteen sixty-five), and helped to build as a plantation through hard work, callused hands, and heartache. It is with deepest regret that I couldn't convince Walter Kinsey of my sincerity. This land, where your ancestors worked while enslaved by my ancestors, will now belong to your family. It in no way repays the debt, or rights the wrongful enslavement of these people, but hopefully the transfer of this property from slave owner's descendant to slave descendant, will help to heal some wounds, and be taken in the spirit given, which is out of the utmost respect for Squire and Molly Kinsey.

To Walter Kinsey III: I leave Twenty-five thousand dollars to be set up in an interest earning account for use when he graduates from high school, toward his college education.

Two weeks after submitting her rough draft to the attorney, he called to advise that it was ready for signing. After review, she signed the Will in front of witnesses. It was done. She filed a copy in a box clearly marked "Will documents". Funeral arrangements crossed her mind as she closed the box. Her mother had taken so much off the family by leaving detailed instructions. Sylvia would do the same.

Chapter Fifty-Three

Visiting the old ladies became a daily routine for Sylvia. She never tired of their company. She was met at the door one morning by three of them all complaining about the nurse. It'd been six weeks, and they felt that the nurse would no longer be needed.

"She's just in our way!" Miss Kate said "She tries to tell us how to eat and when we can look in on Mary."

"We've been eating just fine for eighty years without her advising us!" Miss Emily added

"I'll speak to her. If you don't need her then she's gone!" Sylvia told them

The three women held hands and giggled like schoolgirls who'd just rid their circle of an unpopular intruder.

"We cooked some peas, baked chicken, and cornbread for dinner. You better have some." offered Miss Sally.

Over dinner, everyone discussed plans for the spring flower gardens. Having much more space gave them plenty of options to plant everyone's favorites.

"Do you girls like touch me not flowers?" Sylvia asked

"We can't find the seed no more. We tried to get some last year but nobody plants them around the apartments." Miss Kate answered

"I have some seed. My neighbor gave me some years ago, and I harvest mine every season. I'll bring you some of mine!"

"Mary, did you hear that? Sylvia's got some touch me not seed."

"We're gonna have so many pretty flowers this year!" Miss Mary answered

"You plantin' vegetables this spring?" Miss Emily asked

"No, I don't think so."

"We'll miss those good vegetables. Maybe we can plant a few, if we can get somebody to dig the beds." Miss Kate suggested

Sylvia knew she might not be able to work the garden by spring, but couldn't discuss the reason with them. She hadn't managed to tell Mechelle and the others at the clinic either. Her decision to deny treatment had been difficult. Most wouldn't understand why she'd choose to accept death so easily. She often wondered if living with Squire for thirty-two years made it easier. He made death seem less frightening, other than his being trapped. His conversations of meeting loved one's in glory, had been a comfort to her during her loss of family. She knew her family would be waiting on the other side, and she felt no fear of dying.

Sylvia helped Miss Mary sort through old photographs, searching for some to display on her bedroom wall. Miss Mary found an old photograph of her son as a happy child, holding her hand. In the picture they were standing on the porch of a lovely home.

"Where was this taken?"

"In front of our house. Right after that, my husband left with a woman he met. I didn't hear nothing from him for six months. He came to get a divorce so he could marry her. My boy had cried all those months for his daddy. When he came he wouldn't even wait for school to let out so he could see him. I never laid eyes on him after that day. He never sent no money neither! I lost that house, sometimes worked two jobs to raise my boy. I never did tell him where his daddy went. He always blamed me. I think he still does."

"Where did he think his father went?"

"He heard us fightin' about that woman. I didn't know he was in the house, and he walked in just when I told his daddy to get out. So he thought I ran him off. He loved his daddy so much. I couldn't let him think he chose that floozy over him too."

"What was his father's name?"

"Carl Miller, same as my boy. He's named after him."

"Is that why you never call him by his name?"

"I never thought about it."

"When did you move to Kinsey?"

"I recall it was about nineteen forty three. The mill opened, and I moved here to take a better job. I worked there many years, and took in ironing for people too. My son didn't like it here. He'd left his friends, and thought his daddy wouldn't find him."

Sylvia gave Mary a hug. "You had a hard time didn't you?"

"It wasn't all bad. We had some good times too."

"Tell me about a really good memory!"

"Christmas was always my favorite. One year Carl wanted him some cowboy stuff. You know, gun holster and hat and all. I had to work overtime and do extra ironing, but on Christmas he was so excited when he opened those boxes. The look on his face was worth everything. I surprised him with a cowboy shirt and boots, too."

"I'll bet he thinks of those times too, Miss Mary."

"I don't know, Honey."

That night, Sylvia sat with her mother's box of old photographs. She hadn't opened the box since bringing it from their home. Now she felt she could go through the photographs. There were many memories in that box. She selected some, which she would have enlarged for other family members. Laying them aside, she'd drop them off later in the week.

While in the mood to take care of details, Sylvia wrote the plans for her funeral.

"After carefully going over all options, I have decided on cremation. I could be buried in the cemetery with the family members, but it would cause everyone to feel obligated on holidays to replace the flowers. I really don't like the idea of being underground, either. A marker can be placed on David's grave, listing my name and necessary dates, if you wish. I would like my ashes to be strewn at the old ferry landing. Whoever wants the responsibility for this, is fine with me! If you wish to hold a memorial service, I don't mind. I would like to request that someone furnish transportation for Miss Mary and the other ladies, if a service is held. That about sums it up for me. I love you all."

Once completed, she folded the paper, and placed it in with the insurance policy. She would also drop a copy off by the funeral home. A note was placed inside with Stephanie's instructions, advising that all funeral papers were on file, and boxed in the house.

Chapter Fifty-four

Easter Sunday, nineteen ninety-nine was two days away, Sylvia noticed on the calendar. She purchased miniature baskets for everyone, and filled them with assorted candies. She'd planned a nice dinner, and invited everyone in the family, her friends from the clinic, and the old ladies.

Stephanie called to say she'd make the dumplings, and would bring cranberry sauce. Mechelle was bringing bean casserole, and Matt smoked a turkey. The old ladies had been preparing for the dinner too, and on Saturday afternoon called to announce they would bring a ten layer chocolate cake, a coconut cake, and two buttermilk pies.

The night before Easter, Sylvia set up tables in the front room, and put out the plates and flatware. She prepared dressing, potato salad, and deviled eggs. Totally exhausted, she went to the porch with a glass of lemonade in hand.

"Squire, I'm tired!"

"You been workin' hard in de house! Who all dem tables fo'?"

"Everyone's coming tomorrow for dinner. The family, people from the clinic, and the four old ladies!"

"I wants a see dem ole women. All dem fokes comin' see us! Ain't dat nice. Massa ustah have big parties. Lotsa foke come. Dey wus so much food an' pertty dresses. Miss Amy, she bringed us some dat food an' tole Molly everything what went on."

"Well, tomorrow you can be here to see what goes on for yourself!"

Everyone filed in by eleven o'clock. Ariel was so pretty in her pale yellow dress, and white shiny shoes. She spotted her gift right away.

"Thanks, Aunt Sylvia! This is the best bunny I ever got! He's yellow, just like my dress!"

"You're so welcome sweetheart. Come give me a big Easter hug!"

Introductions were made, and plates were filled with food. Just as the dinner prayer was beginning, someone knocked at the front door.

"Come in" Matt said as he opened the door. "Sylvia, someone's here."

She walked into the hallway, and invited the guest into the front room.

"Mama" he said

Miss Mary turned to find her son standing behind her chair. He walked around, knelt down, and hugged her frail little body, while crying.

"I'm sorry, Mama. All those years, I blamed you! You could've told me the truth. I hated you for him not being allowed to stay with me. I didn't know, Mama. Please forgive me. I do love you."

Miss Mary reached into her apron and retrieved a tissue. She wiped her tears, then Carl's.

"Son, you were such a good little boy. I didn't want you to think he left you too. You believed just what I wanted you to believe. I thought it was best for you. You loved him so much. Ain't no reason for you to apologize to me, Carl."

"Carl, please join us for dinner." Matt offered as he wiped his eyes.

"Thanks. Mama did you bake this cake?"

"I sure did, son. You be sure and get you a piece."

It was a wonderful celebration, full of conversation, laughter, and new understanding. After dinner, Carl called Sylvia aside.

"I thank you so much for this. Since your call, I've done nothing but remember all the mean things I've said to her over the years. I can't take those things back, but I can be a better son for as long as she has left on this earth."

"I'm sure she'll love that, Carl."

By the time the last dish was washed, Sylvia was in severe pain. She told Deborah and Matt to go home; that she needed to rest.

"Sylvia, you're a good old girl, you know. I never knew you were so good at mending fences." Matt said

She knew what he meant. It was his way of saying she'd done a good thing with Carl and his mother. She thanked him.

Matt walked out on the porch to leave, then turned back toward the door, where Sylvia stood.

"Sis, I'm glad they have Mom and Dad's house."

"You're going to turn soft on me Matt!" Sylvia said smiling.

Chapter Fifty-Five

The pain and nausea were worse. Some mornings, Sylvia couldn't get out of bed. Deborah traveled to Kinsey, after telephoning and hearing her voice. When she arrived, she found Sylvia in bad shape.

"Come on now, we're going to the hospital!" Deborah urged

"I will not! Just call Dr. Kendall and see what he can prescribe."

"I know you think you can handle this at home, but I can't stand to see you like this!"

"I'll be okay. Just call him, please Deb."

Dr. Kendall prescribed something for the nausea, and aspirin with codene for the pain.

"There may come a time when something stronger will be necessary. If that happens, call me. I see these patients everyday, and I respect Ms. Champion's decision. I'll be happy to prescribe whatever is needed in the future, to help keep her as comfortable as possible."

"Thank you so much." Deborah said

After taking several doses of the medication, Sylvia did feel better. By August, she knew her time was getting close, and talked with her friends. The old ladies, though upset that she was dying, understood her decision to die as she wished. Mechelle didn't understand, but realized that she would soon loose her best friend, and wanted no hard words exchanged between them. Marty and Richard were supportive, but terribly shocked by the sudden news.

Stephanie was visiting more often, as Sylvia worsened. She wouldn't eat unless coaxed, and then only broth, or a little juice. She refused a nurse, and would wait for Stephanie's visits, if she needed anything. One afternoon, she knew the time had come to have the conversation concerning her last wishes.

"Stephanie, I've made you executor of my Will. It will be read after the memorial service. There are instructions in the top drawer of my chest of drawers. I want you to read them now. I also have a letter to Walter Kinsey, and all the papers he left on the porch that day. He's to get those, along with the cedar box and all contents, except one unopened letter from David. You take that letter. I wrote everything I knew about Old Squire and Molly, and included some of his stories. That journal is in the chest, also. Hopefully Walter will read it, and realize that this old lady wasn't so crazy after all. I'd like for you to take care of giving the chest of things to him, after the Will is read. No one else has to see it."

"Aunt Sylvia, don't make me talk about this!"

"I didn't say talk, I said read. Now get the instructions."

Stephanie found the instructions, and went to the porch to read.

"You must locate Walter Kinsey. He and his son need to be present for the reading of my Will. (Don't ask; I won't discuss this!) Locate him ahead of time so you'll know where to reach him on short notice. He's with the fire department in Fairview, South Carolina. Explaining to your dad the day of the reading, may be difficult. Do the best you can. Just tell him I'm mending more fences. Please visit Squire when I'm gone. You shouldn't have a problem. He's usually around, and can come to you in the yard out to the highway edge. Everything else is spelled out in the will. I love you so much. You've been a delight in my life! Aunt Sylvia"

Stephanie folded the paper, and tore it into several small pieces. She went back to her Aunt's bedside.

"I'll handle everything, Aunt Sylvia. I tore up the instructions, so no one else will see them."

"I think today might be best, Steph."

"What?"

"You need to make some calls, today."

After two calls, Stephanie obtained work and home numbers, and an address for Walter Kinsey. She showed the numbers to her Aunt then placed them in a drawer.

"Thank you honey. I want you to go home now. I'm feeling a little better, and I need to sleep. Come give me a hug before you go. I love you, Stephanie."

"I love you more, Aunt Sylvia."

Stephanie turned off the lights, locked the doors, and left.

At ten thirty p.m., Sylvia called to Squire.

"I's here, Chille. Been here all long since you be gettin' so sick. What wrong? You gone leave Ole Squire, ain't ya? What I gone do now, widout my frien'?"

The old man began to ring his hands and moan to himself. His face was sadder than Sylvia had ever seen.

"Squire, remember when Daddy died, and Mom had to fuss at me for worrying about myself?"

"I members. I know it time of happiness fo' you, not sad. You goin' a see de Lawd. I wants a be glad fo' ya. I ain't doe', Chille! We all to one nuther. Been all long time now! Don't leave Ole Squire! Please Chille, don't leave me! Lawd, what I gone do?"

"Squire, I'm leaving this place to your grandson. I hope he'll move here, or at least visit now and then. Then you won't be alone. You'll have your family nearby."

"Don't bleeves dat'! He ain't never come back since walkin' out de' yard. Ain't gone come see me. I don't wants a be here no moe'!"

"I know you don't. I'm sorry I've failed you. So many times, I tried to find a way to help you leave. Remember? I never could find a way. If I get to glory, I'll talk to the lord and make him understand. I'll see Molly, and tell her you're here. I don't know what else to do."

She was dying. The medication was wearing off, and the pain worsened. She closed her eyes for a moment then hearing a noise by the bed, looked to see that Old Squire was sitting in the chair by her bed.

"Squire, you're sitting down!"

"Sho' is! Did'n' even know I wus. Why I done jest sit down aftah all des' years?"

"I don't know."

He sat there talking, as she moaned and struggled with her pain. She knew death was at hand, and closed her eyes once more, preparing to accept it. Suddenly, she opened her eyes and reached for the pad and pen on the nightstand. With shaking hand, she left a note.

"Squire, I have an idea." she whispered

"Lay still, Chille. Don't you worry none. I gone be fine. Don't worry bout me. I sorry what I said to ya."

"Listen to me! There's no time to argue with you. Hold my hand! You can do it if you try. The lord let you sit down, surely he'll let you hold my hand!"

Old Squire reached his old wrinkled hand forward, and touched hers.

"I can feels yo' hand, Chille!" he yelled

"I'm taking you with me, Old Squire. You hold on tight and when I go, maybe you can go with me."

"You bleeve reel hard, an' I gone bleeve hard too. Wait Chille! I gots a stand up outah dis' chair. Ole Squire gone march into glory! Does I look awrite?"

He brushed off his old tattered coat, straightened his faded shirt, and stood up tall! With hands outstretched, he held hers with all of his might.

"Sang wid' me" he said "We autah be sangin' when we's marchin' in dem' gates, Chille."

"Swang low, sweet chariot, comin' fo' ta carry me home."

Sylvia joined in with weak voice.

"Swing low, sweet chariot, coming for to…"

There was light. Bright white, glowing rays of light were filling the room. Hand in hand they walked into the light, and through it's warmth.

"You sees her, Chille? It my Molly! Sho' is my Molly runnin' a meet me! Ain't she so pertty, Chille? Molly? I's comin' to ya. I's home, Molly. I's finally home!"

Estimated time of death was midnight. Stephanie found the body the next morning. She gathered the papers, called her dad, then the funeral home.

"Squire? Squire?" she called "I know you're sad, but I'll come to see you. I promise I will!"

She called several times, but got no answer. He wasn't there. He was free!

"Aunt Sylvia?" she called "Just checking."

Walking to the bedside to cover her Aunt, Stephanie found the note, "Squire's with me."

With tears streaming down her face, she went into the spare bedroom. Opening the cedar chest, she found the old yellowed envelope. She slipped her Aunt's note inside, with Mrs. Cotton's old note, written in shaky handwriting, "Take care of Old Squire."

"She did Mrs. Cotton. She really did!"

The End

Made in United States
Troutdale, OR
10/15/2024